D1647951

Pride and Prejudice

A Sentimental Comedy in Three Acts

by Helen Jerome

A SAMUEL FRENCH ACTING EDITION

SAMUEL FRENCH

FOUNDED 1830

New York Hollywood London Toronto

SAMUELFRENCH.COM

ISBN 978-0-573-61426-2   Printed in U.S.A.   #854

PRIDE AND PREJUDICE

STORY OF THE PLAY

The play concentrates on Mrs. Bennet's determination to get her daughters married. Jane, Elizabeth and Lydia are likely-looking girls in an unlikely-looking period when a woman's one possible career is matrimony. To be a wife was success. Anything else was failure.

Jane and her Mr. Bingley and Lydia with her Mr. Wickham are quite content with the god of things as they are; not Elizabeth! She actually refuses to marry Mr. Collins whom she openly deplores and Mr. Darcy whom she secretly adores.

The play is the story of the duel between Elizabeth and her pride and Darcy and his prejudice. Each gives in before the evening is over, and pride and prejudice meet halfway.

Copy of program of the first performance of "PRIDE AND PREJUDICE" as produced at The Music Box, New York:

Max Gordon

Presents

PRIDE AND PREJUDICE

A Sentimental Comedy in Three Acts

Dramatized by Helen Jerome from
the novel by Jane Austen

CHARACTERS

(In the order of their appearance)

MR. BENNET	*Percy Waram*
HILL	*Harold Thomas*
MRS. BENNET	*Lucile Watson*
LADY LUCAS	*Frances Brandt*
CHARLOTTE LUCAS	*Brenda Forbes*
JANE BENNET	*Helen Chandler*
ELIZABETH BENNET	*Adrienne Allen*
LYDIA BENNET	*Joan Tompkins*
MR. DARCY	*Colin Keith-Johnson*
MR. BINGLEY	*John Halloran*
MR. COLLINS	*Harold Scott*
AMELIA	*Edwina Wise*
MR. WICKHAM	*John D. Seymour*
BELINDA	*Kathleen Moran*
AMANDA	*Gail Bolger*
A YOUNG MAN	*Hugh Nevill*
CAPTAIN DENNY	*James Jolley*
MISS BINGLEY	*Nancy Hamilton*
AGATHA	*Jeannette Chinley*
A SECOND YOUNG MAN	*Ferdi Hoffman*
A MAID	*Dare Wright*
MAGGIE	*Choteau Dyer*
MRS. GARDINER	*Viola Roach*

5

LADY CATHERINE DE BOURGH..........*Alma Kruger*
COLONEL GUY FITZWILLIAM........*Stephen Appleby*
MRS. LAKE .... *Dorothy Scott*

SYNOPSIS

ACT I

SCENE I. *The drawing room of the Bennet home at Longbourn in Hertfordshire, afternoon.*
SCENE II. *The same, some weeks later, evening.*

ACT II

SCENE I. *The same, a week later, morning.*
SCENE II. *Aunt Gardiner's home at Cheapside, London, a month later, afternoon.*
SCENE III. *Lady Catherine de Bourgh's drawing room, Rosings Park, Hunsford, Kent, a few days later, morning.*

ACT III

SCENE I. *Drawing room at Longbourn, two days later, morning.*
SCENE II. *The same, two weeks later, morning.*

Pride And Prejudice

ACT ONE

Scene I

Scene: *The living room at Longbourn. A large, deep, comfortable room, shabby and used. The fireplace down·Right is crackling with logs, with an overhanging mantel above it and a large family portrait of a man with side whiskers adorning the space over it, as well as other portraits scattered on the other walls. In front of fireplace stands a small bench, and near it a comfortable sofa, facing the audience. In the Right wall, above the fireplace, is a door leading to Mr. Bennet's study.*

In the upstage wall, Right Centre, large double doors lead to the main hall of the house.

In the upstage Left corner, colored French windows open on the conservatory, outside which can be seen the trees and flowers of the garden.

In a corner down Left is another small fireplace, Mr. Bennet's own particular nook, flanked by two large, comfortable chairs.

Disposed about the room are various small tables, including Mrs. Bennet's sewing table, Centre, near a comfortable chair.

The furniture is not of one style or period but gives the impression of having been accumulated over a space of years. A table with lamp above fireplace. An empire drop front desk in upper Right corner; a wire front commode in hall; a spinet up Centre; a small table or stand down Left; a chair down Right. Peacock table in conservatory. Bell pull Left of Right Centre door.

AT RISE: MR. BENNET *is sitting in easy chair below small fireplace* L., *reading a book and smoking his pipe.* HILL, *the butler, enters* R.C. *with bucket of coal and in placing some coal in grate makes a noise which disturbs* MR. BENNET.

BENNET. Hill! You know I don't like to be disturbed while reading.

HILL. Yes, sir.

BENNET. Hill! Take this book to the library. I don't want Miss Lydia to read it.

HILL Very good, sir. *(He exits* R. MRS. BENNET *enters excitedly* R.C. *from* L.; *crosses to* MR. BENNET; *stands back of chair opposite his.)*

MRS. BENNET. My dear Mr. Bennet, have you heard the news?

BENNET. I have not.

MRS. BENNET. It's of tremendous importance to all of us.

BENNET. Can't it wait until I finish this chapter?

MRS. BENNET. No. This means more than any book that has ever been written. The great house at Netherfield has been let at last.

BENNET. Not really!

MRS. BENNET. Yes, it's true. Mrs. Long has just been here and told me. *(He looks unimpressed and continues to patiently survey her.)* Don't you want to know who has taken it?

BENNET. You want to tell me. I have no objection to hearing it.

MRS. BENNET. Well, my dear— *(Sits opposite* BENNET*)* he's a young man of large fortune from the North of England. He's already installed with a retinue of servants.

BENNET. What's his name?

MRS. BENNET. His name is *Bingley*.

BENNET. Married—or single?

MRS. BENNET. Oh, single, my dear, to be sure. With four or five thousand a year! What a splendid thing for one of our girls!

BENNET. How so—how can it affect them?

MRS. BENNET. Mr. B., how can you be so tiresome? You must know that I am thinking of his marrying one of them.

BENNET. Is that his design in settling here?

MRS. BENNET. *(Impatiently)* Design? Nonsense. It's quite likely that he will fall in love with one of them, so you see you must visit him as soon as possible.

BENNET. I see no occasion for that. You and the girls may go—or you may send them by themselves. That may be wiser—for you are as handsome as any of them. Mr. Bingley might like you the best of the party. *(Chuckles.)*

MRS. BENNET. My dear, you flatter me. But when a woman has three grown daughters it's time she gave over thinking of her own beauty. But you *will* call on Mr. Bingley—at once?

BENNET. Oh, come now—that's going rather far. You know my habits.

MRS. BENNET. Mr. Bennet, do you *never* think of your daughters' futures? Do you realize that with our estate entailed they will be practically penniless when you die? To think of that odious cousin of yours—that Collins.

BENNET. *(Suddenly remembering)* Oh, I've had a letter— *(Reaches in his pocket.)*

MRS. BENNET. *(Interrupting)* Now, Mr. Bennet, don't try to change the subject. We're not talking about letters—we're talking of Collins—odious creature!—inheriting our home! You entailing your estate away from your own daughters.

BENNET. Is it really impossible for you to grasp the fact that the Law of Entail was not of my devising, Mrs. Bennet? *(Slowly, as if talking to a child)* The Law dictates that all estates shall be inherited by male descendants only, and we have no son, as possibly you remember.

MRS. BENNET. Mr. Bennet, how can you criticize me? You have no compassion on my nerves. *(Whimpering.)*

BENNET. You are mistaken, my dear. I have a high regard for your nerves. I have heard you mention them with consideration for these last twenty years.

MRS. BENNET. Yes, but you don't know what I suffer. *(Whimpering through this speech.)*

BENNET. That's right, my dear, have a nice little cry. It always seems to help your nerves. *(After a slight pause,* HILL *enters* R.C. *from* R.*)*

HILL. Lady Lucas and Miss Lucas, madam. *(He exits* R.C. *to* R.*)*

BENNET. Oh, good Lord! I think I'll go out and get some air—my horse needs exercising. *(Rises, crosses above* MRS. BENNET, *then comes back a step; pats her on the shoulder)* I'll be back in half an hour—for tea. *(Exits down stage door of conservatory up* L.*)*

MRS. BENNET. Back for tea. Let him miss his tea. It will do him good. *(She rises as* LADY LUCAS *and* MISS LUCAS *are ushered in* R.C. *from* R. *by* HILL. *She crosses to them)* Oh, how nice! I have been pining to see you. *(She kisses* LADY LUCAS. *To* HILL*)* Find the young ladies, Hill, and then tea. *(Sits in chair at table* C. HILL *exits* R.C. *to* L.*)*

LADY LUCAS. *(Crosses to fireplace* R.*)* Let me get near the fire. I am positively frozen. We only have a few moments to spend with you.

MRS. BENNET. Have you heard about our new neighbors?

LADY LUCAS. Yes, we have met the young man, Mrs. Bennet. Charming, perfectly charming! Charlotte is quite smitten with him, aren't you, my love?

CHARLOTTE. *(Has crossed to back of sofa)* Oh, it's no use being smitten—the moment he sets eyes on Jane!

MRS. BENNET. Yes, we'll really have to get Jane out of the way. (JANE *and* ELIZABETH *enter* R.C. *from* L.)

JANE. Who's going to get me out of the way? ⎱ *(Almost simul-*
ELIZABETH. Not if I can prevent ⎰ *taneously.)*
it. Lady Lucas! Hello, Charl!
(They curtsey to LADY LUCAS, *then go over and kiss* CHARLOTTE.)

LYDIA. *(Comes flying in* R.C. *from* L. *as* ELIZABETH *is kissing* CHARLOTTE) Hullo, everybody! (MRS. BENNET *cautions her to remember her manners.)* I mean good afternoon. Mama, did you hear? (MRS. BENNET *shushes her.* LYDIA *crosses to back of sofa.* ELIZABETH *and* CHARLOTTE *cross to fireplace* R.)

CHARLOTTE. *(As they are crossing)* How do you like my new bonnet?

ELIZABETH. I think it's sweetly pretty.

MRS. BENNET. Girls, Lady Lucas has met Mr. Bingley. (CHARLOTTE *sits on chair down* R. ELIZABETH *sits on bench.)*

LADY LUCAS. Sir William had already met him in London and is delighted with him. Young, handsome, extremely agreeable—and *rich,* my dears! (HILL *enters* R.C. *from* L. *with tea tray and sets it on the table* C. *Exits* R.C. *to* L.)

MRS. BENNET. *(Begins to pour tea)* I simply must insist that Mr. Bennet calls tomorrow.

LADY LUCAS. You'll have to wait a few days. He has gone up to London on business.

MRS. BENNET. *(Over her shoulder as she continues to pour)* Are you sure?

LADY LUCAS. Certainly. He was to dine with us yesterday and we received a note of regret that he was called to London. Charlotte was *so* disappointed. (JANE *takes tea from* C. *table.*) Weren't you, dear?

CHARLOTTE. *(Who is conversing with* ELIZABETH*)* Oh—er—yes, Mama. (JANE *serves tea to* LADY LUCAS *and* CHARLOTTE.)

MRS. BENNET. Indeed! But I can't imagine what he can have to do in London so soon after his arrival in Hertfordshire. (JANE *goes back to tea table.*) I do hope the young man won't be flying about from one place to another instead of settling down at Netherfield as he ought.

ELIZABETH. *(Laughing)* Surely, Mama, he has a right to go to London if he wishes? (JANE *hands plate of sandwiches to* LYDIA, *which* LYDIA *serves.*)

LADY LUCAS. He only went for the night. He may be back today. He's giving a ball at Michaelmas.

MRS. BENNET. *(Anguished)* I *must* get Mr. Bennet to call— (JANE *serves tea to* LYDIA *and sits on sofa.*)

LADY LUCAS. He is bringing his sister Caroline back with him. She is to keep house. Also a Mr. Darcy, squire of Pemberly, a princely estate. He is even wealthier than Mr. Bingley, and they are inseparable friends.

MRS. BENNET. Also a bachelor?

LADY LUCAS. Yes, but reported to be engaged to his cousin, the daughter of the Lady Catherine de Bourgh.

MRS. BENNET. I never believed in marriage between cousins. The engagement is *only* a report, Lady Lucas?

LADY LUCAS. Yes, so far. But he's a very high and mighty young man, Mrs. Bennet. He wouldn't look at anyone under a peer's daughter. His mother was the Lady Anne Darcy, sister of Lady Catherine de Bourgh. Oh—very old family!

MRS. BENNET. *(With satisfaction)* Then Charlotte is not in the running either.

ELIZABETH. Mama! Please!

LADY LUCAS. *(Sweetly)* You forget, dear Mrs. Bennet, that since Sir William was knighted by His Majesty, Charlotte has been presented at court. (CHARLOTTE *and* ELIZABETH *exchange looks.)*

MRS. BENNET. *(Still more sweetly)* Mr. Bennet was *born* a gentleman, dear Lady Lucas. Isn't it fortunate for us? My girls don't need to be presented.

JANE. *(Rises and going to* LADY LUCAS. *Anxious to change subject)* Lady Lucas, do let me give you some fresh tea.

LADY LUCAS. *(Rising)* No, thank you, dear. *(All* GIRLS *rise.* LADY LUCAS *hands* JANE *her cup;* CHARLOTTE *hands* LYDIA *her cup;* JANE *hands* LYDIA LADY LUCAS' *cup, which* LYDIA *places on* C. *table.)* Come, Charlotte, we have other calls to make.

MRS. BENNET. *(Inquisitively)* On any mutual friends, Lady Lucas?

LADY LUCAS. *(Evasively)* Oh, only the Longs and perhaps the Hamiltons—

CHARLOTTE. *(As she kisses* JANE. *She then kisses* ELIZABETH*)* Dear Jane.

LADY LUCAS. *(To* JANE*)* Ah, my child—I wish Charlotte had been endowed with a quarter of your good looks— *(To* JANE*)* You'll certainly be the belle at the Bingley Ball. *(Turning to* MRS. BENNET*)* Though it is true that sometimes men prefer character. Goodbye, Mrs. Bennet. *(Curtsies to* MRS. BENNET. CHARLOTTE *curtsies to* MRS. BENNET. LADY LUCAS *and* CHARLOTTE *cross to the* R.C. *door.)*

MRS. BENNET. *(Curtsies to* LADY LUCAS*)* Goodbye, Lady Lucas.

LADY LUCAS. Goodbye, my dears. Thank you for the delightful tea. *(They exit* R.C. *to* R.*)*

MRS. BENNET. *(Sits) Well!* What a cat that woman is! Men prefer character, do they? *(JANE crosses to place cup on tea table.)*

ELIZABETH. I can't say I have noticed it. *(Pause)* But if she means that our Janie lacks it—that's her mistake.

LYDIA. *(Crosses to table C. with plate of sandwiches)* Oh, she's only jealous. Poor Charlotte was squirming all over.

JANE. *(Standing R. of MRS. BENNET)* Oh, she doesn't mean anything. Perhaps I haven't any character. As long as you all love me, I don't mind.

⌐ ELIZABETH. *(Crosses to JANE, kisses her, gives her cup which JANE places on tea table)* You have the loveliest character in the world, darling.

JANE. *(As she is placing cup on table. ELIZABETH crosses to sofa.)* Mama, weren't your eyes a little bit red? *(Goes over and kisses mother)* You weren't crying before the Lucases came, were you?

MRS. BENNET. Yes—your papa. Of all the selfish, inconsiderate men, disobliging, cantankerous! *(Sighs.)*

ELIZABETH. *(Sits on sofa. The GIRLS laugh.)* What unspeakable thing has he done—this time? *(Walks up.)*

MRS. BENNET. Refuses to call on Mr. Bingley. For no reason in the world.

ELIZABETH. *(Slyly)* Did you *ask* him to?

MRS. BENNET. Of course!

ELIZABETH. And you call that *no* reason? Why, don't you know *yet* that men instinctively *refuse* everything we ask them to do—and end by doing it?

JANE. *(Wonderingly)* But that doesn't sound sensible—

ELIZABETH. Who *said* that they were sensible? I'll wager that Papa is on his way to Netherfield at this very moment.

LYDIA. Well, who cares whether we meet Mr. Bingley or not? I don't, for one. I prefer men in uniform—military ones.

ELIZABETH. Oh, yes. Army officers are always excellent companions. You can talk to them and be thinking of something else at the same time.

LYDIA. I don't see why.

ELIZABETH. I can't imagine any intelligent man voluntarily choosing a regimented life— (LYDIA *crosses back to conservatory windows; looks out.)*

MRS. BENNET. Really, Lizzy! I can't imagine where you get your queer ideas— But what makes you think your father—

LYDIA. *(Who is looking out of the window, goes up steps by window)* Well, upon my word!

JANE. What is it?

MRS. BENNET. *(Rises and goes to* LYDIA*)* Lydia, you shouldn't be staring out! *(Goes to window and stares out)* Why, it's your father—and two gentlemen! *(Excitedly. Turns to* ELIZABETH*)* Good gracious, Elizabeth, you're uncanny. I believe they're our new neighbors.

ELIZABETH. *(Laughing)* You see, one can always tell what they will do.

JANE. *(Goes to* ELIZABETH; *takes her hands)* Lizzy, how clever you are!

MRS. BENNET. *(Coming* R.C. *with* LYDIA*)* Oh, my dears, and none of you dressed in your taffetas. *(The* GIRLS *primp.* MRS. BENNET *straightens* LYDIA.*)*

BENNET. *(He and* DARCY *and* BINGLEY *are seen in conservatory.* HILL *meets them and takes* DARCY *and* BINGLEY'S *wraps, which he places on peacock table in conservatory. He then precedes the others through the* C. *door of conservatory and exits* R.C. *to* L. BINGLEY *stands* L. *of* MRS. BENNET *and* DARCY L. *of* BINGLEY.*)* Mrs. Bennet, let me present our new neighbors—Mr. Bingley, my wife; Mr. Darcy, my wife, and my daughters— *(Names them "Miss Jane,"*

"Miss Elizabeth," "Miss Lydia." As he names them
DARCY *comes down* C. BINGLEY *stands at foot of
steps.)* Have you some tea left for us, Mrs. Bennet?

MRS. BENNET. I'm all of a tremble— Lydia, ring
for Hill, my love! So charmed, my dear sirs!

DARCY. Your servant, ma'am! (LYDIA *rings for*
HILL; *stays upstage, bored with the proceedings.*
DARCY *crosses to chair below* R. *fireplace and stands
in front of it.)*

BENNET. *(After a pause)* I was riding to Netherfield to call on these gentlemen and actually met them
en route to the village— *(Crosses to fireplace* L.;
warms hands. GIRLS *laugh.)* But—what's so funny
about that? *(As the* GIRLS *laugh—even their mother.)*

MRS. BENNET. *(Gushing, to* BINGLEY*)* Never
mind! It *is* so nice to have some eligible young men
in the neighborhood at last, Mr. Bingley. (BINGLEY
takes a step to L. *of table* C.) I hope we shall see you
often this winter?

BINGLEY. *(Eyes on* JANE*)* I think I can promise
that, ma'am. (BINGLEY *crosses to sofa.* HILL *enters*
R.C. *from* L. *with fresh tea. Replaces other teapot.*
MRS. BENNET *sends him off* R.C. *to* L. *with a gesture.)*

ELIZABETH. *(Who has been watching her mother,
crosses to* DARCY*)* I hope you are finding our part
of the country to your liking, Mr. Darcy.

DARCY. *(Turning to her with a stiff bow)* I do not
care for the country, Miss Bennet.

ELIZABETH. What a pity! Then it must irk you to
be compelled to live in it. Lady Lucas was telling us
of your estate at Pemberly. (BENNET *takes small
chair from* L. *fireplace, moves it to* L.C. *and sits.)*

MRS. BENNET. What? Not care for the country,
sir? Surely you don't prefer London to Derbyshire?
*(*JANE *crosses to tea table.)*

DARCY. One moves in such a confined circle outside
big cities.

MRS. BENNET. Indeed! Well, I for one don't agree

with you. The only advantages big cities have over us is their shops. It's true we can't buy anything we really want in the High Street at Meryton—it certainly upsets me at times—

DARCY. Does it? *(He bows to her with the sort of attention that would insult an intelligent person. ELIZABETH crosses to back of sofa. LYDIA exits R.C. to L.)*

MRS. BENNET. *(To BINGLEY)* I hear from Mrs. Long that your drawing-room has *such* a charming prospect over the gravel walk. I really don't know a place in the county to equal Netherfield for its view. You'll not think of leaving us in a hurry, I hope, even though you have only such a short lease?

BENNET. I see you've not been idle, Mrs. Bennet.

BINGLEY. *(JANE takes tea from table; serves BINGLEY.)* Everything I do is done in a hurry. *(Laughs)* When I fall in love I expect it will be the same. *(Looks at JANE, who drops her eyes, embarrassed. She moves away from him and serves DARCY.)*

DARCY. *(Crosses to sofa; sits)* That isn't anything to boast of, my dear fellow. *(DARCY half rises as he takes tea from JANE. JANE hands him tea.)* Thank you, Miss Bennet. It's a sign of a far from solid character.

ELIZABETH. *(Cuttingly to DARCY)* Thank goodness for that. Mr. Bingley seems far too charming for solidity.

BINGLEY. *(Loooking at her with pleasure)* You begin to understand me, Miss Bennet?

ELIZABETH. Perfectly.

DARCY. Is that a compliment— *(ELIZABETH looks at him questioningly, her eyebrows slightly raised.)* —to be so transparent?

ELIZABETH. In this case—yes. It is not always the deep people who are the charming ones. *(JANE serves BENNET; stays at his chair.)*

BENNET. Charming ones often cause the most trouble, though.

DARCY. So—you are a student of character, Miss Bennet?

ELIZABETH. *(Very quietly)* At times.

DARCY. But you must have little opportunity to exercise your gift here?

ELIZABETH. On the contrary, sir.

DARCY. I am of the opinion that those who live in the country—belong to the country.

BINGLEY. Well, as for me, I like 'em both. City or country, wherever I am I'm happy. Give me a horse, a long road, a whiff of hay— (JANE *takes plate of sandwiches from table; serves* BINGLEY *just as he says:)* —and a country rose! (JANE *meets his eyes.)*

MRS. BENNET. That is because you have a nice disposition, Mr. Bingley. *(Unmistakable emphasis on the "you")* That gentleman seems to think that green fields are beneath him. *(Indicates* DARCY.)*

JANE. *(Hastily)* Indeed, Mama, you misunderstand Mr. Darcy. He only means that city people are different from us. May I give you some more tea, Mr. Darcy? *(Takes two steps toward* DARCY. *He rises.)* I am sure yours has grown cold.

DARCY. Thank you very much. It is to my liking. I rarely drink it warmer. *(He crosses to chair down* R.; *sits.* JANE *places plate on table above fireplace.* BINGLEY *looks after her as she comes back to sofa.* ELIZABETH *suggests by gesture she sit on sofa.* JANE *then sits on* R. *end of sofa.)*

MRS. BENNET. You know Sir William Lucas, I believe, Mr. Bingley?

BINGLEY. *(Sitting on sofa)* Yes, ma'am. He was one of the first gentlemen of the county to honor me with a visit.

MRS. BENNET. What an agreeable man! So much the man of fashion—so genteel and easy—always something to say to everybody. *That,* Mr. Bingley, is *my* idea of breeding. So unlike those people who fancy themselves too important to open their mouths except to criticize. (ELIZABETH *crosses and sits on bench* R.)

BENNET. It might be well to give them less cause, Mrs. Bennet. (MRS. BENNET *turns to look at him.*)

ELIZABETH. I'm sorry you were not here earlier, Mr. Bingley. My friend, Charlotte Lucas, was here—

MRS. BENNET. *(To* BINGLEY*)* Mr. Bingley, it is really tragic that poor Charlotte is so plain.

BINGLEY. She seems a very pleasant young woman.

MRS. BENNET. *(With sad sweetness)* Oh, yes, very. But her face—

BENNET. *(Rising.* DARCY *and* BINGLEY *rise.* GIRLS *also rise.* JANE *takes cup from* DARCY.*)* Mrs. Bennet, what about releasing the gentlemen to come to the library for a glass of Madeira wine? *(To* MRS. BENNET*)* That homicidal feeling is creeping over me that invariably attacks me at tea parties.

BINGLEY. *(Hands teacup to* JANE; *takes step to* BENNET*)* That is very good in you, sir, but we must be getting back to Netherfield. My sister is alone.

MRS. BENNET. *(Rises)* You mustn't believe that Mr. Bennet really wishes to murder my guests, sir. He is not such a bear as he pretends. *(Turning to* BENNET *and shaking her finger at him)* If you continue to say things like that the gentlemen will begin to pity me.

DARCY. *(Who has crossed to bow before her)* Indeed, ma'am, we should never dream of pitying *you.* (DARCY *crosses up behind* BINGLEY; *turns; bows to* GIRLS. *They curtsey.*)

BINGLEY. Your servant, ma'am! I trust we may look forward to your visit to Netherfield very soon— (ELIZABETH *whispers to* JANE. MRS. BENNET *curtseys*) —with your daughters. My sister is impatient to receive you.

MRS. BENNET. Tell Miss Bingley we shall call to-morrow. *(Blithely)* I want to be quite certain of securing you both for our little assembly next month.

BINGLEY. Oh, that's most kind of you, ma'am.

MRS. BENNET. *(Gasps from the family.)* We usually give our ball about this time. *(Starts with BINGLEY toward doors of conservatory. BENNET and GIRLS exchange looks of amazement.)*

BINGLEY. We shall be prodigiously pleased to come, you may rest assured of that, ma'am. (BENNET, DARCY, MRS. BENNET and BINGLEY exit through conservatory.)

JANE. *(Crosses and places cup and saucer on table c. To ELIZABETH)* Whatever is Mama talking of?

ELIZABETH. *(Excitedly. Crosses to JANE)* Jane! He likes you!

JANE. Likes me? Why, Lizzie—whoever do you mean?

ELIZABETH. I don't mean Mr. Darcy—for I doubt that he likes anyone—with the probable exception of himself. But Mr. Bingley—there's a gentleman of rare intelligence and perception. From the first moment he laid eyes on you he could look at no one else. I approve of him for that.

JANE. *(Laughing)* Ah, my darling Lizzie—for all the worldly wisdom that you delight to assume, you have a truly romantic heart.

ELIZABETH. *(Indignantly. Takes off jacket)* What? Never have I been so insulted!

JANE. Do not dare to deny it. And some day some man will discover it and he will make you love him—desperately—marvelously!

ELIZABETH. *(Crosses to chair down R.)* Perhaps, my sweet. But I haven't yet met the man who could inspire so much as a flicker of interest. *(Places jacket on chair.)*

JANE. Not Mr. Darcy?

MRS. BENNET. *(Enters from conservatory; crosses*

to table c.) That Mr. Darcy! What a disagreeable, horrid man! So high and conceited— Dear me, there was no enduring him!

JANE. *(Crosses to* MRS. BENNET*)* But what a darling Mr. Bingley is!

MRS. BENNET. Quite the gentleman! I flatter myself you made quite an impression on Mr. Bingley.

BENNET. *(Enters from conservatory)* Nothing to the impression you made on Mr. Darcy, Mrs. Bennet.

MRS. BENNET. I have no desire to impress such an ill-bred young man. I don't want his admiration.

BENNET. *(Replaces small chair to* R. *of fireplace* L.*)* Well, that sounds like a veritable coincidence to me.

MRS. BENNET. What an excellent father you have, my dears! I don't know how you will ever repay him for his kindness—or me either, for that matter.

LYDIA. *(Entering* R.C. *from* L.*)* Well, has His Royal Highness departed? Heavens, I hope I never meet such a conceited prig again!

MRS. BENNET. *(Crosses to* LYDIA*)* Ah, Lydia, my love, where did you get to?

LYDIA. I couldn't stand the majestic atmosphere of Mr. Darcy, Mama. He made me feel much too inferior.

MRS. BENNET. Well, never mind. Even though you are the youngest, you're just as pretty as Lizzie. Mr. Bingley is sure to dance with you at our ball—

LYDIA. Our ball? What ball, Mama?

MRS. BENNET. The one your papa and I are giving next month. (LYDIA *hugs her and gives an exclamation of delight.)*

BENNET. *(Crosses to* L.C.*)* Thank you for the news of my intentions, Mrs. Bennet. But may I crave a little further information?

JANE. Why don't you tell us beforehand of your intentions, Mama?

Mrs. Bennet. Well, I only knew it myself just before I said it.

Bennet. I may be unduly inquisitive, Mrs. Bennet—but may I ask who is going to pay for this nonsense?

Mrs. Bennet. You, of course, you silly man! How do you ever expect me to find husbands for your daughters if you persist in being so stingy with me?

Lydia. You must invite all the officers from Colonel Forster's regiment, Mama. I'll give you their names.

Mrs. Bennet. *(Firmly)* Only those with private incomes, my dear. It's just as easy to fall in love with one of them. (Lydia *pouts as the* Others *laugh.*)

Bennet. *(Crosses to fireplace* r. *back of bench)* Now, Mrs. Bennet, I have a surprise for *you.* I have a confession to make.

Mrs. Bennet. *(Crosses to front of sofa)* Confession! Mr. Bennet, what *have* you been up to?

Elizabeth. Mama expects the worst— Never mind, Papa, I'll stand by you.

Bennet. Well, it's about that letter— *(To* Mrs. Bennet*)* I received it a week ago—and I *did* try to tell you about it this afternoon, but as usual, I couldn't induce you to listen— It was from a gentleman— (Elizabeth *crosses back of bench and takes* Mr. Bennet's *arm.*)

Mrs. Bennet. *(Crosses to sofa)* I suppose in your own good time we shall know *what* you are talking about.

Bennet. I hope you have an extra nice dinner for this evening, my dear.

Mrs. Bennet. *(With dignity, sits on sofa)* The dinners I serve you are usually excellent, Mr. Bennet. But *why* this evening specially? (Jane *crosses to chair* c.; *sits.* Lydia *crosses and sits on arm of same chair.*)

Bennet. Because we are about to have an addition

to the family circle for a few weeks. Our guest may arrive any time now—

Mrs. Bennet. Mr. B.—you will be the death of me with your slow way of telling things. A guest— May one ask the gentleman's name?

Bennet. Mr. William Collins— (Girls *evince interest and astonishment.*) My cousin; you know, the popular gentleman who may turn you all out as soon as he pleases when I am dead.

Mrs. Bennet. How you love your little jokes, my dear! As if that odious creature would have the impudence to show his face here— I can't bear to think of Collins coming and taking my home when you die. If it were not for the entail I shouldn't mind it.

Bennet. Now if you listen a moment—I will tell you his reason for inviting himself—your heart may be softened.

Mrs. Bennet. Indeed, it will not! I think it very impertinent of him to invite himself—and very hypocritical—and I shall be very reserved with him—very reserved indeed! *(They* All *roar at the idea of any reserve from her.)*

Bennet. In his letter he hinted—only hinted, mind you—that he wishes to look over our daughters with the object of choosing one for a wife—so that he can partly atone for the guilt of inheriting our estate.

Mrs. Bennet. *(Interested at this)* Then he must have *some* proper feeling?

Elizabeth. Can he be a sensible man, sir?

Lydia. He sounds to me a bit of an ass. *(Crosses so she is* c. *on her next speech.)*

Mrs. Bennet. Now, Lydia, my love, is that a nice way to speak of a clergyman? (All *laugh at her sudden change of front.)*

Lydia. I thought I heard you refer to him as an odious creature a few minutes ago, Mama? *(Continues cross until she is back of sofa.)*

BENNET. That, my dear, antedated his becoming a matrimonial prospect.

HILL. *(Opens* R.C. *door; enters; stands in the doorway)* Mr. Bennet, sir!

MRS. BENNET. *(Rises; crosses* L. *of* HILL*)* Oh, Hill, we are expecting Mr. Collins for dinner, and to stay for several weeks—

HILL. Quite, madame. And I was going to say, sir— *(To* BENNET*)* I showed the gentleman to his room as you directed—as soon as he arrived.

MRS. BENNET. *(To* MR. BENNET, *agitated)* Arrived— (JANE *rises.)* Already? Why, Mr. Bennet! Is that— (JANE *crosses around to* L. *of table; faces* R.C. *door.)*

HILL. *(Goes to door)* It *is* the gentleman, ma'am. Mr. Collins. *(Exits* R.C. *to* L.*)*

(COLLINS *enters* R.C. *from* R. *with a grave, stately air and ridiculously formal manners. He bows to* MRS. BENNET *and swings, bowing to include* ALL *in one sweeping bow.)*

BENNET. *(Crosses to* COLLINS*)* Ah, Collins, at last! (BOTH *men bow formally but very friendly.)* You can't imagine how interested your letters have made me in this meeting—

COLLINS. Your most obedient, sir! *(Bows several times.)*

BENNET. *(Introductions)* Mrs. Bennet, let me present the Reverend Mr. Collins, our esteemed cousin. My wife, sir, and my daughters: Miss Jane, Miss Elizabeth, Miss Lydia. (COLLINS *bows to each in turn; very low to* MRS. BENNET. *The* GIRLS *curtsey.)*

COLLINS. I have been long anxious to come. *(Turns to and includes the* OTHERS. *To* MRS. BENNET*)* I am grateful, ma'am, that my overtures were so graciously accepted by you.

MRS. BENNET. *(Gushingly. Escorts him to sofa; sits)* Not at all, dear Cousin. We have looked forward to this happy occasion.

COLLINS. *(Starts to sit; notices* GIRLS *are standing; motions them to be seated, then he sits)* I must compliment you, ma'am, on so fine a family of daughters. I had heard much of their beauty, but in this instance fame falls far short of truth. There is no doubt that you will soon see them well disposed in marriage.

MRS. BENNET. It *is* so kind of you to say that, Cousin. Indeed— *(Sighs)* I hope so, for they will certainly need rich husbands. Things are arranged so very oddly.

COLLINS. *(Guiltily)* You doubtless allude to the entail of the estate, ma'am? *(Look between* BENNET *and* ELIZABETH.*)*

MRS. BENNET. Ah, sir, 'tis indeed a grievous affair—not that I blame *you.* Far from it! We all know who is to blame. (MRS. BENNET *looks knowingly at* BENNET; *he places his finger to his lips to caution her to be quiet.)*

COLLINS. Indeed, I am very sensitive of the hardship to my fair cousins. *(Bows toward the fair ones)* But—I have come—with a *plan. (Surveys the* GIRLS, *his head on one side. As he looks at each girl she modestly lowers her head)* Perhaps when we are better acquainted— *(He looks intently at* JANE, *who shrinks back in her chair.* MRS. BENNET *directs his attention to* ELIZABETH.*)*

MRS. BENNET. *(Rises; crosses up)* Oh, Mr. Collins, I must go to see that Hill is getting out some of Mr. Bennet's better Port. Come, Lydia, and help me. (LYDIA *exits* R.C. *to* L. MRS. BENNET *backs to* R.C. *door on this last line.)*

COLLINS. You are hospitality itself, dear Mrs. Bennet.

MRS. BENNET. And in the meantime, dear Mr.

Collins, do proceed with your plan. (MRS. BENNET *exits* R.C. *toward* L.)

BENNET. *(Coming down to sofa, sits)* According to your letters you seem to be prodigious fortunate in your patroness, Cousin.

COLLINS. *Ah!* The Lady Catherine de Bourgh?

ELIZABETH. *(Half to herself)* Lady Catherine— de Bourgh!

COLLINS. *You* know her ladyship, Cousin?

ELIZABETH. Only by name, sir. We do not mingle with such exalted society at Meryton.

COLLINS. Do not be downhearted, Miss Elizabeth. Stranger things have happened, I assure you. And when you do meet Her Ladyship, believe me, you will agree that it is the greatest of privileges. (ELIZABETH *nods gravely.*) She has actually invited me to dine at her mansion, Rosings, *twice,* and sent for me only last Sunday to make up her pool at Quadrille. Yes, indeed! Her Ladyship is considered proud and haughty by many people, but I have seen nothing but affability and condescension.

BENNET. Does Her Ladyship live near you?

COLLINS. *(Lyrically)* The garden in which stands my humble abode is separated only by a lane from Rosing Park. *(WARN Curtain.)*

BENNET. You certainly are blessed, sir!

COLLINS. *(Modestly)* I try to remain worthy of my good fortune, sir. I often observe to Her Ladyship that her charming daughter seemed born to be a Duchess. These little remarks please a mother who is nobly born—and it's the sort of attention I feel it my duty to pay.

BENNET. You certainly have a high sense of duty. (COLLINS *bows with what he trusts is a proper humility.*) May I ask whether it comes naturally, or do you think it out?

COLLINS. *(With a deprecating air)* No, it is quite natural with me, sir! *(DRESSING BELL rings.)*

JANE. *(Rising.* COLLINS *rises. The* GIRLS *rise.* BENNET *rises and goes back of sofa.)* Oh, the dressing bell. We dine at seven-thirty, Mr. Collins!

COLLINS. *(Crosses to* JANE *and walks with her to* R.C. *door)* After dinner, my dear cousins, if you care for it—I am considered a very good reader—I will gladly read aloud to you as we gather round the fire.

ELIZABETH. *(Crosses to* COLLINS; *crosses up with him and* JANE *to* R.C. *doors)* Oh, that will be entrancing! We have a vast deal of novels.

COLLINS. *(Turns—shocked; wounded) Novels!* Oh, my dear cousin! I never read such works. *(Brightly)* But I have brought with me an excellent volume of Fordyce's Sermons! *(Offers* JANE *his arm.* BENNET *and* ELIZABETH *exchange glances.* BOTH *laugh. He gives* ELIZABETH *his arm and apes* COLLINS *as they exit* R.C. *to* L.*)*

MEDIUM CURTAIN

ACT ONE

SCENE II

SCENE: *Same as Scene I. Some months later. Lighted candles are set on mantelpiece over fireplace* R. *and on pedestals in conservatory. Also in hallway. MUSIC is playing off stage.* MRS. BENNET'S *"little assembly" is taking place.* AMELIA *and* CAPTAIN DENNY *enter* R.C. *from* L.

AMELIA. How warm it is in the ballroom! I am pining for a drink of something cool.

CAPTAIN DENNY. *(Serves drink from punch bowl on table up* R.*)* Then it is my privilege to offer it to you.

LYDIA. *(Bounces in* R.C. *from* L.*)* Oh, my dear Miss

Amelia! Oh, my dear Captin Denny! Did you *ever* in your lives have such an utterly delightful time?

CAPTAIN DENNY. Never, Miss Lydia! 'Pon my honor!

AMELIA. It has been charming.

LYDIA. Oh, I know my own mama and papa are giving the ball and I shouldn't run on about it so. But I can't help it. I really can't.

CAPTAIN DENNY. And why shouldn't you? Some shrub, Miss Lydia?

LYDIA. *(Glancing off* R.C. *to* L.*)* N—no— Papa says I mustn't. He says it's too strong. *He* thinks I'm a child.

AMELIA. Papas are *all* like that. Shall we return to the ballroom, Captain Denny?

CAPTAIN DENNY. By all means! *(He and* AMELIA *go out* R.C. *to* L. *Alone,* LYDIA *glances off* R.C. *to* L., *then goes to the punch bowl and snatches a quick one.* WICKHAM *comes in from the conservatory; sees her; pauses on the steps. She puts the glass down hastily.)*

LYDIA. Mr. Wickham!

WICKHAM. Your servant! *(He comes down)* But there's something most grievously wrong here.

LYDIA. Wrong?

WICKHAM. That you should be alone for an instant! It is a reflection on the intelligence of every gentleman present that one so young and so surpassing fair should lack an escort.

LYDIA. Ah, Mr. Wickham! You officers talk as beautifully as you look.

WICKHAM. Our lives of grim duty make us doubly appreciative, Miss Lydia. *(He looks about)* After the rigors of camp life, it is sheer delight to find oneself in such elegant company in so fine a house.

LYDIA. You must see many houses that are finer.

WICKHAM. There are not many that bespeak so

much of quiet gentility. A perfect setting for so
exquisite an ornament as—

LYDIA. As what, Mr. Wickham?

WICKHAM. Need I say it, Miss Lydia?

LYDIA. Why—yes—I think you might—

WICKHAM. Your father is a wealthy man, Miss
Bennet. But I should say that his greatest treasure
is his youngest daughter.

MRS. BENNET. *(Enters* R.C. *from* L. *with* LADY
LUCAS*)* My dear Lydia—and my dear Mr. Wickham.

WICKHAM. Your servant, ma'am. (LYDIA *curtseys to* LADY LUCAS.)

MRS. BENNET. Have you seen our conservatory,
Mr. Wickham?

WICKHAM. Yes, ma'am—I have just been admir-
ing—

MRS. BENNET. *(Paying no attention)* Do take
Mr. Wickham to see our conservatory. We have
some—some tropical things of some kind— I can
never remember those dreadful Latin names—but
they're peculiarly fine specimens.

LYDIA. *Do* come, Mr. Wickham. *(MUSIC stops.)*

WICKHAM. With the utmost pleasure. *(They exit
into conservatory.)*

MRS. BENNET. Think of it! My youngest daughter,
and virtually at the marriageable age! Isn't it incredible?

LADY LUCAS. With three daughters, you must find
yourself in a permanent state of incredibility.

MRS. BENNET. *(Beaming. MUSIC starts.)* I know!
It makes life so entertaining, doesn't it? Will you
have some shrub, Lady Lucas? Mr. Bennet promised
me it would be *most* harmless. (AGATHA *and* 2ND
YOUNG MAN *come in from conservatory with greetings.)* Ah, my dears, do go in and dance. The
musicians become so discouraged if everyone stays
in the conservatory. *(They go out* R.C. *to* L. *Comes
down* C.*)*

LADY LUCAS. *(Crosses to* MRS. BENNET*)* Such a well-behaved young lady!

MRS. BENNET. Yes, I like her prodigiously. She's not a bit pretty.

LADY LUCAS. I've noticed how fond you are of my Charlotte.

MRS. BENNET. *(Actually embarrassed)* Oh, Lady Lucas—indeed you must not feel that way. Dear Charlotte is such a sensible girl.

LADY LUCAS. *(Dryly)* That means it's going to be difficult to find her a husband— *(Quietly)* You should know how little regard gentlemen have for *sense* in young ladies—dear Mrs. Bennet—

MRS. BENNET. You see, I'm not much of *an authority* on such matters—I was married so young.

LADY LUCAS. *(Half to herself)* Yes, I know that.

MRS. BENNET. Ah, to be young again! Mr. Bennet is not a bit romantic! Don't you think our husbands—

ELIZABETH. *(Enters* R.C. *from* L *with* CHARLOTTE. *Stands just below* R.C. *door)* Tippling, Mama? And you, Lady Lucas? Shame on you! (LADY LUCAS *steps up stage.)*

MRS. BENNET. There's nothing in this, Lizzie. Your dear papa promised.

ELIZABETH. Then my dear papa must have been a bit absentminded when he made the mixture. It's violently potent.

MRS. BENNET. Oh, dear Lady Lucas, perhaps we'd best not finish our cups. *(Crosses to spinet, finishing hers before she sets goblet down.)*

ELIZABETH. Your guests are awaiting you, Mama.

MRS. BENNET. Charlotte, my dear—I do hope you'll be particularly nice to Mr. Darcy.

CHARLOTTE. As nice as I may be, Mrs. Bennet.

MRS. BENNET. *(To* LADY LUCAS, *as they go out* R.C. *to* L.*)* None of *my* girls can *abide* him!

ELIZABETH. Is it not a relief to get away from all

those dancing dervishes? Will you have some of this shrub, Charlotte? *(Places fan on table* c., *her scarf on chair; goes to punch bowl.)*

CHARLOTTE. *(Crosses to table* c.*)* Mr. Bingley was saying what a good idea it was to have it away from the supper room "where a fellow could have his tipple in peace." Nice young gentleman, isn't he?

ELIZABETH. Quite charming! Jane seems to think so too. How lovely the darling looks tonight. Her eyes are like stars. I wonder if her shyness is such an asset, though?

CHARLOTTE. You fear Bingley might need encouragement?

ELIZABETH. Few men possess enough heart to be really in love without it, Charl.

CHARLOTTE. I imagine Bingley will get the needed encouragement this evening. He seems to be enjoying himself immensely.

ELIZABETH. I hope so. For myself, I call it deadly dull. All I can see is a number of brainless young men and eager young ladies prancing about awkwardly to the strains of tepid music. Do you think this sort of thing is fun, Charl? *(Crosses to chair below* L. *fireplace; sits.)*

CHARLOTTE. *(Crosses to chair opposite* ELIZABETH ; *sits)* It's a means to an end. Surely, Miss Caroline Bingley is warning enough against spinsterhood.

ELIZABETH. Is a warning necessary?

CHARLOTTE. Did you notice the fair young Lydia's triumphant progress in the ballroom—right under the maternal nose too, and your mother just beamed on her.

ELIZABETH. Yes. Mama is shocked if a gentleman glimpses our ankles, but to let him understand that he may attain complete possession is perfectly proper.

CHARLOTTE. *(Rubbing her feet)* Dear me, my feet ache.

ELIZABETH. What do you think of that new man,

Mr. Wickham? Very attractive, isn't he? *(MUSIC stops.)*

CHARLOTTE. *(Feeling one of her slippered feet tenderly)* That delectable Collins trod all over me.

ELIZABETH. But are you trying to evade my question, Charlotte?

CHARLOTTE. About Wickham? I noticed Miss Bingley refused to stand up with him.

ELIZABETH. *(Mocking the proper* DARCY*)* I expect she models herself on Darcy and only stands up with members of the peerage.

CHARLOTTE. *(Laughs)* To be quite sincere—I feel there's something not "right" about this Wickham. *(Looks searchingly at* ELIZABETH*)* Don't waste your time, dear. Concentrate on Darcy—rich, aristocratic—

ELIZABETH. *(Rises)* —priggish and snobbish—

CHARLOTTE. Well, we must take what offers, my dear. When do we ever meet the knights of our dreams? Men were put into the world to teach women the law of compromise.

ELIZABETH. *(Laughs; rises)* Don't be ridiculous, Charlotte. Come, we must speed the few remaining guests. (CHARLOTTE *rises; goes to* ELIZABETH. *MUSIC starts.)*

AMANDA. *(Entering* R.C. *from* L. *with* YOUNG MAN*)* Oh, Miss Elizabeth!

ELIZABETH. I'm vastly sorry you are leaving, Amanda.

AMANDA. *(Crosses to* CHARLOTTE*)* It has been a truly delightful evening. Shall I see you tomorrow, Charlotte?

YOUNG MAN. We can go out this way. The carriage is near this door.

ELIZABETH. Oh, we'll see you out.

AMANDA. It was a most excellent ball.

CHARLOTTE. I saw you going down the dance hall. All the gentlemen were struck with you. *(Ad lib. as*

they exit. As they go out into conservatory, DARCY
comes on R.C. *from* L., *followed by* BINGLEY. DARCY
crosses to up L.C.)

BINGLEY. *(Enters; crosses to punch bowl; takes
goblet of punch)* Darcy! What are you thinking of?
The evening is nearly over. You must dance. Come,
be a good fellow.

DARCY. *(Crosses to fireplace* L.; *leans on mantel)*
I realize that I am not contributing much to the gaie-
ty of the assembly. But it is difficult to "be a good
fellow" on such an occasion.

BINGLEY. *(Crosses to* R. *of* DARCY) But aren't
any of the young ladies to your taste?

DARCY. I should call them all uncommonly pretty.

(ELIZABETH *and* CHARLOTTE *appear in conservatory.)*

BINGLEY. And Miss Jane is the prettiest of all.
Really, Darcy, you're notoriously lacking in apprecia-
tion, but did you ever behold anyone more exquisite-
ly lovely?

DARCY. If you wish me to agree with you, I shall
be glad to do so.

BINGLEY. And what of her sister? She's quite
pretty, too.

DARCY. Miss Elizabeth?

BINGLEY. Yes.

DARCY. She is the one above all others that I
prefer to avoid.

BINGLEY. But, really—she is most agreeable.

DARCY. On the contrary, she is one of the most
disagreeable young women I have ever had the ill-
luck to encounter.

BINGLEY. Shame on you, Darcy. *(Takes him by
the arm)* She is a delightful girl. Find out for yourself.

DARCY. *(Submitting and going toward* R.C. *door
with* BINGLEY. BINGLEY *places empty glass on table*

up R.) Oh, very well—for your sake. But I'll only stand up with her once. *(The* GIRLS *get out of view as they pass them on way to door.)*

BINGLEY. You may change your mind. (DARCY *and* BINGLEY *exit* R.C. *to* L.)

ELIZABETH. *(Enters with* CHARLOTTE *indignantly through French windows)* Why do we tolerate that man? (CHARLOTTE L. *of* ELIZABETH. ELIZABETH *crosses above* C. *table.)*

CHARLOTTE. *(Crosses to table* C.*)* No doubt because he is of the very rich. Those who do not envy the tribe, adore it.

ELIZABETH. *(Crosses to large fireplace)* Well, I shall see that he does not come here again.

CHARLOTTE. You forget, dear, that he is the bosom friend of Bingley and may influence him against Jane.

(ELIZABETH *is about to reply when they* BOTH *turn toward* R.C. *door as* WICKHAM *enters agitatedly.)*

WICKHAM. *(Enters* R.C. *from* L.; *comes down in front of sofa)* Oh, Miss Elizabeth, I was looking for you to bid you goodnight. I am leaving at once. (GIRLS *look at each other in surprise.)* You'll excuse me, something very unpleasant—

ELIZABETH. *(Rather stiffly)* Unpleasant? *Here?*

WICKHAM. I would rather not talk about it.

ELIZABETH. But, Mr. Wickham, I insist!

WICKHAM. Just now in the ballroom, Mr. Darcy—

ELIZABETH. Mr. Darcy? What has he done?

WICKHAM. Your mother wished to present me to Miss Bingley. Mr. Darcy was with her at the moment. They declined to be introduced and walked away.

ELIZABETH. This is beyond bearing— But why— I was not aware that you had even met before?

WICKHAM. We knew each other only too well—

CHARLOTTE. And yet he declined to meet you? There usually is some reason for a gentleman to refuse to meet a fellow guest.

ELIZABETH. A gentleman would have more consideration for his hostess.

WICKHAM. I am not qualified to form any opinion of Mr. Darcy. I have known him too long—and too well—to be a fair judge.

ELIZABETH. But, Mr. Wickham, why did he offer you such an affront?

WICKHAM. Please do not ask me, Miss Bennet. I do not wish to injure him in your eyes. If you will permit me I shall say goodnight. *(Crosses to* ELIZABETH *and bows)* He might come in. I would not subject *you* to a repetition of the disgraceful scene in the ballroom.

ELIZABETH. Indeed he would never dare.

CHARLOTTE. But may I ask why you are so anxious to avoid him, Mr. Wickham?

WICKHAM. *(Turning to* CHARLOTTE*)* I have no reason except a sense of very great injustice. I wish to spare him the embarrassment of meeting me.

ELIZABETH. *(Sits on bench)* Injustice! I am full of sympathy.

WICKHAM. *(Sits on sofa)* You are so kind, Miss Elizabeth—   *(MUSIC stops.)*

ELIZABETH. Tell me, where did you know him?

WICKHAM. My father was manager of the Darcy estate in Derbyshire.

ELIZABETH. Oh!

WICKHAM. When the elder Darcy died he left instruction that his son should bestow upon me a sum of money.

CHARLOTTE. May one ask why, Mr. Wickham?

WICKHAM. I was his godson—he was very fond of me. I was also to receive the clerical living in his gift at Pemberly.

ELIZABETH. But surely, Mr. Darcy obeyed his dead father's wishes?

WICKHAM. He refused me both the living and the money.

ELIZABETH. The wretch!

WICKHAM. I was forced to enter the army—a life I detest.

ELIZABETH. But what can have induced him to behave so cruelly?

WICKHAM. A determined dislike of me which I can attribute only to jealousy.

ELIZABETH. Indeed, I do not like Mr. Darcy. I could hardly have believed him dishonest.

CHARLOTTE. And I should have thought him too proud to be.

WICKHAM. Thank you for your sympathy, Miss Elizabeth. It has been very precious to me. You will forgive me for inflicting all this upon you, but your heart is so kind. Please let me go now. Convey my apologies and regrets to Mrs. Bennet— I will go this way. *(Rises, kisses her hand, looks at R.C. door, then, pointing to conservatory, exits up L.)*

ELIZABETH. *(Stands staring after him, then turns. Crosses behind sofa to between table and the door R.C.)* There's a sample of Darcy for you!

CHARLOTTE. *(Crosses to L. of C. table; picks up book)* I don't like emotional men—it seems to me that the reserve of Darcy is preferable. Surely, Lizzie, there must be two sides to this affair. *(MUSIC starts.)*

ELIZABETH. Yes, a right and a wrong. *(Angrily.)*

DARCY. *(Enters R.C. from L.; comes down to ELIZABETH)* Oh, Miss Elizabeth, they are playing the last extra. May I have the honor? *(Approaches ELIZABETH and offers arm.)*

ELIZABETH. Thank you, sir, I am too tired to dance any more. (DARCY *is surprised at the refusal. Takes two steps down to table* C.) Besides, I fear the honor would be more than I could bear.

DARCY. Have I had the misfortune to offend you?

ELIZABETH. It is rather Mr. Wickham whom you have offended, sir—one of my mother's guests.

DARCY. It is more than he merits, ma'am.

ELIZABETH. I beg your pardon. I found him very charming, and I am sure my mother did.

DARCY. He is blessed with the charm that makes *new* friendships. I doubt if he possesses the quality to retain them.

ELIZABETH. *(Moving away indifferently, crosses to sofa.* DARCY *looks at her.)* He certainly lacked the talent to retain yours. (ELIZABETH *smiles at* CHARLOTTE, *who crosses, sits in chair* R. *of table, smiles at* ELIZABETH *and begins to read book.* ELIZABETH *sits on sofa.* DARCY *and* ELIZABETH *look at* CHARLOTTE *as she sits in chair.* DARCY *then gazes intently at* ELIZABETH. *She turns and sees, then speaks, after a pause)* Did you enjoy the music, Mr. Darcy?

DARCY. Very much, thank you. *(Crosses to bench in front of* R. *fireplace.)*

ELIZABETH. *(After another pause)* It's your turn to make a remark now.

DARCY. Whatever you wish me to say, you may consider said.

ELIZABETH. Very well. I daresay there *are* times when perhaps it is better to limit conversation to yes or no.

DARCY. *(Quietly)* Are you consulting your own wishes—or do you imagine that you are gratifying mine? *(MUSIC comes faintly off stage.)*

ELIZABETH. *(Looking over at him defiantly)* Both—I recognize our similarity. We are each unsociable and taciturn—reluctant to speak unless we can say something that will astonish the whole room or be handed down to posterity. *(She smiles at him during the last part of this speech.)*

DARCY. *(Unbends when he sees her smile)* I hardly think that describes your character, Miss Bennet. You are probably describing mine and include yourself out of pity for my wounded feelings.

ELIZABETH. Have you any, Mr. Darcy? (CHARLOTTE *gives her a quick look of remonstrance.)*

DARCY. Evidently you have *decided* about that— *(Looks away from her.)*

ELIZABETH. *(Facing him)* I hear such different accounts of you—I am puzzled. When you are present, some of the reports seem—difficult to believe.

DARCY. *(To her, haughtily)* Why bother to try to solve the puzzle? It's much easier to—

MISS BINGLEY. *(Enters* R.C. *from* L., *her wraps on, ready to leave)* Oh, are you ready, Mr. Darcy? Almost everyone has gone. (ELIZABETH *rises; crosses to* MISS BINGLEY.) *You* haven't danced much, Miss Bennet.

ELIZABETH. No, there was a scarcity of gentlemen and I preferred to leave them for our guests. I trust you had plenty of— *(Looking at* DARCY *and back at* MISS BINGLEY*)* partners, Miss Bingley? Won't you sit while waiting for your brother? *(Offers her seat on sofa.* BOTH *sit.)*

MISS BINGLEY. Thank you. I expect he'll come here for me. *(Pause)* You danced a good deal with Mr. Wickham. I didn't know he was a friend of yours. How did you ever meet him? (DARCY *crosses to back of bench.)*

ELIZABETH. He came here with Colonel Foster. He is a very interesting young man and seems a gentleman.

MISS BINGLEY. What curious taste you must have, Miss Elizabeth!

ELIZABETH. *(Rises)* We are speaking of one of my mother's guests, Miss Bingley. *(Crosses to between sofa and chair.)*

MISS BINGLEY. *(Looks at DARCY)* I hear you are quite delighted with him. Did you know that his father was merely a steward on the Darcy estate—a sort of servant? (DARCY *turns away in distaste at the trend of the conversation.)* No doubt he told you that Mr. Darcy had injured him?

ELIZABETH. *(Looking at DARCY)* He did. (MISS BINGLEY *looks at* DARCY. *He meets her glance, then looks away.)*

MISS BINGLEY. Do let me caution you not to give too much credence to his tales. The truth happens to be just the contrary. *(She waits for some reaction from* ELIZABETH*)* I am sorry you must be disillusioned. But what can you expect, considering his origin?

ELIZABETH. *(Steps toward her)* That seems to be his chief fault in your eyes, Miss Bingley. People don't arrange their origins in advance—nor have I observed that the well-born are invariably the well-bred. *(Slowly and meaningly)* I think perhaps you attach too much importance to the accident of birth. *(Turning away from her, crosses to behind chair* c.*)*

MISS BINGLEY. Accident? Really, Miss Bennet!

ELIZABETH. *(Turns to* MISS BINGLEY*)* Didn't you ever learn any biology?

MISS BINGLEY. I hope I was never so unfeminine! (CHARLOTTE *and* ELIZABETH *exchange glances. With distaste)* I'm told you are clever—and read books on subjects that only belong to gentlemen. Well, it won't get you very far. *(Looks at* DARCY.*)*

ELIZABETH. When you speak of "getting far," I suppose you refer to marriage with one of them?

MISS BINGLEY. Certainly. And you are going the wrong way about that, I assure you; men detest clever women.

CHARLOTTE. Well, why did you let them discover how clever *you* are, Miss Bingley? *(Rises; curtseys to* Miss Bingley, *then to* Elizabeth*)* I must get my wraps. Are you coming, Lizzie? *(Goes out* R.C. *to* L. Darcy *bows to* Charlotte *as she curtseys.)*

Elizabeth. I'll tell your brother you are waiting for him. *(Curtseys; exits after* Charlotte.*)*

Miss Bingley. *(Very angry)* Ill-bred young woman! I can imagine what you are thinking, Mr. Darcy.

Darcy. *(Staring out into space. Dryly)* I doubt it.

Miss Bingley. *(Softly)* Oh, yes—we are too much alike for me not to *feel* your disgust at such people. That Elizabeth! Forward—over-educated. I am longing to get home to Netherfield to hear you hold forth on the family.

Darcy. I was really thinking of what beautiful eyes can do in the face of a pretty woman.

Miss Bingley. Who is the lady?

Darcy. Miss Elizabeth Bennet! *(With a slight bow.)*

Miss Bingley. Goodness! I am all astonishment. How long has *she* been in favour? And when am I to wish you joy?

Darcy. Exactly what I expected you to ask. A lady's imagination is so rapid. It jumps from admiration to love and from love to marriage in a moment.

Miss Bingley. Nay, if you *are* serious about it, I shall consider you already married. You will certainly encounter no opposition. *(Looks at him; felinely)* And what a charming mother-in-law you will have!

Darcy. I can allay your fears for my future, Miss Bingley. I have no doubt that Miss Elizabeth Bennet will soon be married, but not to me.

Miss Bingley. I'm glad to hear you say that, Mr. Darcy. For the family is really impossible—the mother especially!

(BINGLEY *and* JANE *walk across* R.C., *above doors,*
L. *to* R.)

JANE. You should have danced more with the
others.

BINGLEY. Dance with the others? When you are
there?

JANE. Charles!

MISS BINGLEY. *(Sincerely concerned)* Have you
noticed Charles? *(Anxiously)* He seems to be fall-
ing in love with Jane. Of course I am very fond of
her. She is really a sweet, dear girl, but my dearest
ambition has always been to see Charles and your
sister Georgiana— I should hate to hurt her, but my
brother's interests come first!

DARCY. I cannot believe he is really serious, but I'll
have a talk with him tonight. I'll go and hurry him.
(Crossing to door R.C. *when* COLLINS *enters* R.C. *from*
L.*)*

COLLINS. *(Twitteringly)* Oh, Mr. Darcy, sir, I've
only just heard that you are the nephew of my
revered patroness, Lady Catherine. *(Bows low)* I
want to apologize for not having paid my respects
earlier. (DARCY *looks at him in astonishment.*) I
am happy to inform you, sir, that your noble aunt
is enjoying robust health. I heard from her only yesterday. She bids me speed my wooing— *(Simpers)*
—and hurry home.

MISS BINGLEY. What wooing, Mr. Collins? Are
you contemplating marriage?

COLLINS. *(Comes down in line with* MISS BINGLEY*)*
It's a secret—as yet, ma'am—but as you are friends
of the family—

DARCY. The family?

COLLINS. It is Miss Elizabeth. I have chosen her
to be mistress of my parsonage.

MISS BINGLEY. May I congratulate you, Mr. Collins? A most suitable marriage! I don't imagine you

will be refused. (DARCY *crosses to back of table* C.) It is no easy matter for girls without connections *or* wealth to find suitable husbands, especially when they are hampered with an over-supply of intelligence.

COLLINS. *(Hastily, crossing to* MISS BINGLEY*)* Oh, you do her an injustice, Miss Bingley. I'm sure my dear cousin is not unsexed with too much brain. *(Shaking head earnestly)* I shouldn't like that at all. you know. *(Bowing profoundly to* DARCY*)* May I hope to see something of you, sir, when next you visit your revered relative? *(Pauses.)*

BINGLEY. *(Enters* R.C. *from* R.*)* Have I kept you waiting?

DARCY. Ah, Charles, here you are at last!

BINGLEY. Awfully sorry, but I have been having such a splendid time!

COLLINS. You will all excuse me but there is a certain young lady who commands my most ardent attention— *(Exits* R.C. *to* L.*)*

DARCY. *(Goes up and stares after* COLLINS. *After a pause, laughs and comes back down* C.*)* Well, I fancy Miss Elizabeth's intelligence will protect her from *that* particular calamity.

MISS BINGLEY. Are we all ready?—I've said good-night to our hostess.

BINGLEY. I'd like a bracer before our cold drive. *(Goes to table and ladles some punch)* Anybody else? *(They shake their heads and watch him drink with gusto, and note his happy air.)*

MISS BINGLEY. By the way, Charles, what was it Jane told you about her uncle?

BINGLEY. *(Reluctantly)* Oh, I dislike speaking badly of a man I've never met—she told me he is— an attorney!

DARCY. Good heavens!

MISS BINGLEY. *(Triumphantly)* And lives at Cheapside— *(She takes* BINGLEY's *arm. She is delighted at* DARCY's *look of horror.)*

BINGLEY. *(Going toward* DARCY *and French windows)* Well, if Jane and Elizabeth have enough uncles to fill all Cheapside it doesn't make them one bit less lovable and charming. *(Through* R.C. *doors we see* AMANDA *and* YOUNG MAN *crossing* L. *to* R.*)*

YOUNG MAN. *(As he crosses)* Did you hear about Mrs. Long, my dear? She came in a hack chaise! *(*HILL *and* MAID *enter* R.C. *from* L.; *business of putting out lights, etc. They exit through French windows.)*

AMANDA. *(As she crosses)* Isn't it shocking? She has not kept a carriage in a twelve month.

BELINDA. *(And* 2ND YOUNG MAN *are seen crossing behind French windows of conservatory)* Oh, yes, Papa is thinking of fixing in town for the season. He is prodigiously fond of superior society.

2ND YOUNG MAN. And how you will adorn it, Miss Belinda!

*(*CAPTAIN DENNY *and* AGATHA *cross in hall* L. *to* R.*)*

CAPTAIN DENNY. It was cruel of you to deny me the happiness of standing up with you.

AGATHA. Not too many protestations, sir. *(During the above,* JANE *and* ELIZABETH *can be heard now bidding the guests "good-night." During general "good-nights.")*   *(WARN Curtain.)*

DARCY. *(As they go toward door)* True, but it does materially lessen their chances of marriage with men of any consideration in the world. *(They ad lib. as they exit through the French window. VOICES are heard off stage: "Goodbye," "It was delightful,"* ELIZABETH *replying. DOORS slam. CARRIAGES heard driving away.* ELIZABETH *and* JANE *enter* R.C. *from* L.*)*

ELIZABETH. Let's see if the fire is nearly out. It isn't safe to leave it burning. *(Goes to* R. *fireplace; takes shovel; fixes fire.* JANE *is watching her dreami-*

ly. JANE *comes down* R. *to end of sofa.* ELIZABETH *crosses to* JANE) Well, darling? You've had a happy time? I've noticed you— *(Tenderly.)*

JANE. *(In a low voice)* Lizzie—I'm too happy! It frightens me!

ELIZABETH. *(Putting an arm around the trembling girl)* My darling—happiness belongs to you. You are so sweet and good— *(Kisses her)* Is it Charles? *(*JANE*, her eyes shining with an expression of tremulous rapture, can only nod.)* Has he made you an offer, dearest?

JANE. Oh, no, Lizzie—you know he will ask my father first, but I *know* he will, oh, I know—

ELIZABETH. One can't always be sure—in these matters— *(Very tenderly)* What makes you so sure?

JANE. *(Suddenly clinging to* ELIZABETH*)* He—kissed—me, Lizzie— *(There is a half sob in her voice as she hides her face on* ELIZABETH'S *shoulder. They embrace and cling together in the emotion of two innocent and tender souls to whom a kiss meant love and love the whole meaning of life. They shed a few little trembling tears and wipe them from each other's cheeks with their doll-like handkerchiefs.)*

ELIZABETH. Well, then, darling, you're as good as married— *(They contemplate each other with wet, shining eyes.)*

MEDIUM CURTAIN

ACT TWO

SCENE I

SCENE: *The same as Act One. Morning. One week later.*

AT RISE: *A cold, damp, typically English morning. The family enter at different intervals by different entrances, having just finished breakfast. They gather here because of the fire crackling cheerfully in the grate.*
"The Times" (newspaper) is folded neatly on a small table near the L. fire, carefully placed by HILL, *who has entered with it at rise. He arranges* BENNET'S *chair, sacred and untouchable, in comfortable proximity to the only paper; pokes up the fire and is bending over it as* LYDIA *bounces in* R.C. *from* L. LYDIA, *with a quick glance at his back, quickly picks up "The Times," gingerly turns its pages, hoping he won't hear them crackle. She is obviously anxious to find a certain page when* HILL, *hearing, turns.*

HILL. Oh, Miss Lydia—I shouldn't—I shouldn't really! *(Approaches anxiously)* The master will be prodigious vexed if his journal is disturbed. *(Worried)* He will be hupset for the rest of the day.

LYDIA. *(Devouring it quickly, one eye on the* R.C. *door)* What he doesn't know won't hurt him.

HILL. *(Respectfully but firmly trying to get pos-*

47

session of the paper) But, Miss, he knows if even a fly walks on it. He can't abear a fussed-up journal. It turns him up if it's the least bit creased.

LYDIA. *(One hand keeping him off, the other holding the paper, reading avidly)* Be quiet, Hill!

HILL. But Miss Lydia, I shall get the brunt of it.

LYDIA. *(Still reading)* Do you good—

MRS. BENNET. *(Enters R.C. from L.; carries wools, work basket, etc. Looking over at* LYDIA *and "The Times")* Oh, Lydia, naughty girl! Put that journal down at once! (LYDIA *obeys nervously but angrily.)* Good gracious, isn't Mr. Bennet cross enough in the morning?

LYDIA. I only wanted to see if there are orders for moving Captain Denny's regiment— I was watching the door— (HILL *nods approval, goes up stage, gets sewing basket, L. of R.C. doors, and brings it down to* MRS. BENNET.)

MRS. BENNET. Well, if he caught the merest glimpse of you even near that table the business would be settled. *(Sighs)* I simply couldn't cope with any more ill-temper for one morning. You'd better fold it exactly as it was— *(Watches* LYDIA *doing this. Sorts out her wools)* I'm sure I don't know what makes men so tiresome at breakfast time.

LYDIA. At breakfast time? *(She has just replaced paper in time and managed to spring away from its vicinity. Walks to French doors up L.* BENNET *enters R.C. from L.* HILL *glances over to make sure paper is in proper place.* BENNET *goes straight to his private chair; opens paper; adjusts his glasses.* MRS. BENNET *looks across at* LYDIA *significantly, indicating the necessity of silence and the danger of disturbing the male in the holy act.* LYDIA *pouts; goes to window; looks out at the chill landscape; turns with a bored expression; speaks in what she fondly believes is an undertone; crosses to sofa)* I do wish I knew where the Regiment was to be stationed, Mama.

MRS. BENNET. Don't waste your time, my love. You are worthy of something more secure than a penniless fellow in a uniform.

LYDIA. Ah, but think how their uniforms show off their dashing figures, Mama!

BENNET. Upon my word, I think you must be quite the silliest creature in the country. I've suspected it for some time. But now I am convinced. (LYDIA *sits on arm of sofa.*)

MRS. BENNET. I am astonished, Mr. Bennet, that you should be so ready to think your own daughter silly. If I wished to think that way of anybody's child it would never be my own.

BENNET. If my children *are* idiots, I hope I am intelligent enough to know it.

MRS. BENNET. You mustn't expect a girl to have as much sense as her mother. I daresay Lydia doesn't think any more of men in uniform than I did at her age. *(Nodding and smiling at* LYDIA*)* I thought Mr. Wickham looked very becoming in his regimentals last week.

(ELIZABETH *and* JANE *enter* R.C. *from* L.; *stay at the door.*)

LYDIA. *(Sits on sofa; eagerly)* Mama, my aunt Phillips says that Colonel Forster and Mr. Wickham are quite often standing in front of Clark's library at Meryton. Couldn't Lizzie and Jane and I walk into the village this afternoon? (ELIZABETH *and* JANE *look at each other.*)

BENNET. *(Looks at* LYDIA*)* For God's sake, go and get something useful to do. Get to your studies and don't let me listen to any more of this foolishness. (MRS. BENNET *nods secretly to* LYDIA *to obey.* LYDIA *goes out sulkily, pouting and swaying her body. Exits* R.C. *to* L.*)*

ELIZABETH. *(Crosses to chair opposite* BENNET*)*
Papa, I think you handle Lydia the wrong way.

JANE. *(Crosses to chair* C. *Gently)* She's only a
baby yet—soldiers are romantic to her.

BENNET. I only hope she'll get more sense as she
grows older, though I doubt that it ever comes if it
isn't born in a female. *(Looks at his wife.)*

MRS. BENNET. *(Thinking it wise to change the
subject. Brightly)* I suppose our dear cousin Collins
is preparing his sermon for Sunday.

BENNET. Are we really to be bereft of his spark-
ling society in a few days? *(Looking across at her)*
You *have* changed your opinion of that young man,
Mrs. Bennet. He still inherits the estate, you know.

MRS. BENNET. *(Looking archly at* ELIZABETH*)*
Ah, but I fancy it's going to stay in the family after
all. He seems enchanted with Lizzie. (ELIZABETH
gives a quick look at MRS. BENNET, *then back to
sewing.)* And what with that and our darling Jane
and Mr. Bingley—

BENNET. *(Surveying her)* You've the whole thing
settled, eh? Do the gentlemen know of your plans?

MRS. BENNET. Don't be so tiresome, Mr. Bennet.

ELIZABETH. Jane, will you walk to
the village with me this afternoon? I
have to get—

MRS. BENNET. Jane, dear, I thought
you were going to see Mr. Bingley— *(Together;
chatting.)*

JANE. Oh, I don't know.

MRS. BENNET. Jane, dear, I think
you really ought to stay home.

JANE. Yes, Mama, I think I will.

BENNET. *(Rises; irritably)* Bah—there's too much
chatter here. I'm going upstairs to read my paper in
peace. *(Exits* R.C. *to* L.*)*

MRS. BENNET. *(As he goes)* Men have no control
whatever over their nerves! (ELIZABETH *laughs.)*

JANE. Papa is only teasing you, Mama. (HILL

enters R.C. *from* R.; *comes down with several letters on his salver.)* Oh, letters!

HILL. *(Hands them to her)* One for you, Miss Jane, two for Miss Lizzie. *(Hands them to her)* One for Miss Lydia—

ELIZABETH. Thank you, Hill.

HILL. *(Looks around)* Shall I take it to her schoolroom, ma'am?

MRS. BENNET. No, give it to me. The child is too young to open her own letters. (HILL *gives her letter.* MRS. BENNET *opens it; chuckles.)*

HILL. There are several for the Master, Ma'am. Shall I take them to him?

MRS. BENNET. Yes, he has gone upstairs. (HILL *exits quickly* R.C. *to* L. JANE *has been reading her letter throughout this. Her face clouds, she stifles an exclamation, at which* ELIZABETH *looks at her and leads her off through library door* R. MRS. BENNET *is reading* LYDIA'S *letter, giggling at its contents.* COLLINS *enters* R.C. *from* L. *As he comes forward with one of his stiff formal bows)* Ah, Cousin, we have missed you.

COLLINS. Thank you, ma'am. But I had two sermons to prepare in readiness for my return to my parish. Now nothing remains to be done before my lamented departure Wednesday except— *(Rather simperingly, hesitates.)*

MRS. BENNET. *(Archly)* I wonder if I can guess! Eh—you naughty boy! *(Shakes finger playfully.)*

COLLINS. Have I your permission—and Mr. Bennet's, of course—to pay my addresses to your fair daughter, Miss Elizabeth, ma'am? *(Bending over her confidentially)* I should like an interview with her this morning, if possible—before I write to my revered patroness—

MRS. BENNET. Nothing would give me greater pleasure, sir. *(Rises; drops her sewing, cottons. spools, etc., as she hastily rises to call* ELIZABETH. *The things roll everywhere.* COLLINS *goes down on all fours to rescue them. He is sprawled under the sofa as he mumbles.)*

COLLINS. Then you will persuade her to grant me a private audience? *(He gets up and hands her the various spools he has salvaged.)*

MRS. BENNET. *(Excitedly)* Yes, yes, my dear Mr. Collins, at once. *(Calls. She looks all around)* Lizzie, my love! Where on earth did my girls go? They were here just now.

COLLINS. Shyness, no doubt, my dear Mrs. Bennet. Miss Elizabeth is avoiding me out of maidenly modesty.

ELIZABETH. *(Enters from library* R.*)* Where you calling me, Mama? (COLLINS *by this time has his head stuck under the couch.* ELIZABETH *looks over couch and sees him)* Oh, Mr. Collins, have you finished your sermon? *(As she notes his idiotic fatuous smirk and her mother's agitation, she fears the worst and makes for the French windows to escape)* If you'll excuse me— *(As he puts out a detaining hand)* I want to reply to this letter from Mr. Wickham. *(Heading for door* R.C.*)*

MRS. BENNET. *(Stops her)* No, Lizzie, Mr. Collins has something to say to you— *(Moves toward* R.C. *door herself, takes* ELIZABETH'S *hand and draws her back. When* ELIZABETH *resists and tries to escape, panic-stricken, she says angrily)* Elizabeth, I desire you to remain here. *(She pulls her over to* L. *of sofa.)*

ELIZABETH. *(Returning reluctantly; protesting through above speech and business)* But Mr. Collins can have nothing to say to me that won't wait, Mama. (MRS. BENNET *close to door, evidently intending to exit.)*

COLLINS. *(Fondly)* It's perfectly understandable and indeed proper that a young girl should display this modesty, my dear Mrs. Bennet. Pray, don't blame your charming daughter. (MRS. BENNET *kisses* ELIZABETH *and backs out of* R.C. *door. Closes door.)* Indeed, Miss Elizabeth, it is an added incentive. *(Plants himself in front of her. She sits, with a sigh of resignation, in chair* C.*)* You can hardly be in doubt as to what I am about to propose, my dear and lovely Elizabeth! *(She turns away from him.)* Your natural delicacy may lead you to dissemble—but I flatter myself my attentions have been too marked to be mistaken. *(He grows more pompous every minute)* I have singled you out as the companion of my future life— *(Waits for her exclamation of wondering gratitude—but she is silent)* And before my feelings run away with me—I owe it to you to tell you the reasons. (ELIZABETH *looks at him questioningly.* COLLINS *nods in reassurance)* That very noble lady, my patroness, has condescended to advise me to marry, and even goes so far as to promise to visit—actually visit—the lady I bring to the parsonage as my wife—if I choose wisely. Another reason, my fair cousin, is that you have the honor of knowing her nephew, Mr. Darcy. The mere fact of your acquaintance with him would do much to recommend you to her favor. And charming and genteel as he is, his manners are as nothing to those of his noble aunt. *(She looks at him.)* You can learn so much from her. These, dear Miss Elizabeth, are my motives. And now nothing remains but to assure you of the violence of my affection. *(He kneels.* ELIZABETH *moves away from him, closer to table.)* I know that one thousand pounds invested at four percent is all you will have as dowry—and—even *that* you will not receive until your mother's death, which lamentable event may not occur for several, nay, many years. *(Pauses)* But you can rest assured that on *that* score no ungenerous word of reproach shall ever pass my lips after we are married.

ELIZABETH. *(She looks down on him. Slowly)*

Aren't you a little hasty, sir? You seem to forget that I have made no answer to this dazzling offer! I appreciate the honor you have done me— *(He raises her hand, which he had to grab for, to his lips. She rises from him so quickly that she nearly upsets him)* —but candor compels me to decline it.

COLLINS. *(Rising slowly with broad grin)* Indeed, I understand, dear Miss Elizabeth— Yes, it is quite a charming and delicate custom for young ladies to say *no* when they mean *yes.* *(Archly, shaking a finger at her)* I am, therefore, not at all discouraged and shall hope to lead you to the altar before very long.

ELIZABETH. *(Astonished and getting exasperated)* Upon my word, sir, you are difficult to discourage. I assure you I am *not* one of those idiotic young ladies you describe, if indeed they exist outside of novels. Difficult as it seems for you to believe—I will *not* marry you.

COLLINS. Come, come, Miss Elizabeth—

ELIZABETH. You could not make *me* happy, and I certainly could not make you so—

COLLINS. Such charming modesty!

ELIZABETH. What is more, I have no ambition to try. *(She crosses toward* R.C. *door. He runs up to cut her off. She then starts* L. *to go out through conservatory. Stops to deliver next line)* And if your friend, the Lady Catherine de Bourgh, really knew me, she would utterly disapprove of me for the exalted position you offer.

COLLINS. *(Suddenly sobered)* Oh—if I thought Lady Catherine would disapprove! *(Reflects; looks her up and down)* Ah, but *no*—impossible! You can be sure that when I have the honor of seeing her ladyship again—

ELIZABETH. You had better ask *her* to choose for you; only select a young woman with a humbler and more contrite heart—

COLLINS. Ah, no, dear Cousin, my mind is made up. And I am too well aware that it is by no means certain that any other gentleman will ever make you an offer—so I naturally understand that your rejection of my suit is according to the usual practice of elegant females.

ELIZABETH. *(Almost bursting into laughter)* I see! Well, if you can, try to stop thinking of me as an elegant female. Just picture me as a *rational* creature with a most inelegant habit of speaking the truth. *(As she crosses to exit* R.C., COLLINS *runs ahead and blocks the door.)*

COLLINS. *(Seizing her hand and kissing it)* Ah, you are quite adorable!

ELIZABETH. *(As she crosses him)* Mr. Collins!

COLLINS. I am quite certain now that when my proposal is formally sanctioned by your excellent parents that you will plainly say yes.

ELIZABETH. No, Mr. Collins, I will as plainly as possible say no. *(She crosses to library door. He tries to get to door. She brushes him aside)* And you need not try to scamper in front of me again. This time I am going out by this door. *(Exits* R.*)*

COLLINS. *(Looks after her)* She loves me! *(He crosses to up* L.C.*)* She loves me!

MRS. BENNET. *(Enters* R.C. *from* L.; *comes down* C.*)* Well—my dear future son-in-law—am I to wish you joy?

COLLINS. *(Bows; crosses to* MRS. BENNET. *With much assurance)* Thank you, indeed I trust I have every reason to be satisfied. *(Indulgently.* MRS. BENNET *almost embraces him—"refusal" stopping her.)* Of course, I know that my cousin's refusal naturally springs from her bashful modesty, and—

MRS. BENNET. *(Alarmed, for she knows her* LIZ-ZIE*) Refusal?* *(Shakes head)* With *her* that does *not* mean acceptance—but—

COLLINS. You think she means it?

MRS. BENNET. Never mind, my dear boy. I'll convince her. *(Half to herself)* Headstrong, foolish girl!—She never knows her own interests! But I'll teach her! *(Forces him into chair C.)*

COLLINS. *(Worried)* Headstrong? Foolish? But, dear me! Those qualities will not make her a very desirable wife! *(Pauses)* If she actually persists in rejecting— *(Rises)* —my suit— I pray you, madam, I pray you—don't force her. I fear if she has those defects—she will hardly succeed in making me happy.

MRS. BENNET. *(Laughs frightenedly)* Oh, no; oh, dear no. The dear child is merely willful in these matters and so shy—you can't imagine. All her life she has run away from admiration. She's a veritable gazelle, I assure you. Just wait a minute! *(She pushes him back into chair)* I will call her papa. He always brings her to reason. *(She exits quickly R.C. to L. But she has finished COLLINS.)*

COLLINS. *(As he paces)* Headstrong? Foolish? *(Goes to bell rope; pulls it frantically. Goes off R.C. to R. to get hat; comes back smiling. He has decided to propose to CHARLOTTE)* Ah— *(As HILL enters R.C. from L.)* I have just remembered a call I promised to make on Sir William Lucas. Will you be good enough to saddle one of your master's horses for me?

HILL. Certainly, sir—the groom was just about to take Ranger for his morning exercise—he is ready saddled. If you will hurry—we can catch him before he mounts— This way, sir— *(They go out quickly through French windows. MRS. BENNET's voice heard even before she enters with BENNET. She is saying: "Oh, Mr. Bennet, we are—")*

MRS. BENNET. *(Off)* Oh, Mr. Bennet! Oh, Mr. Bennet, you're always so slow—we're all in an uproar. Come, come, quickly. You must use your authority. *(They enter R.C. from L. He goes with the aggravating slowness and absence of response to excitement of his type to the* L. *fireplace to warm his back; watches her amusedly.)* Why, he has gone! Oh, my dear, you *must* do something. *(Calls)* Elizabeth! *(Tearfully)* Lizzie refuses to marry Mr. Collins! You must force her to change her mind— You must make haste, Mr. Bennet—or he will change his and not have her. *(Goes to him.)*

BENNET. I have not the pleasure of understanding you. May I ask what you are talking about?

MRS. BENNET. Of Mr. Collins and Lizzie. Lizzie declares she won't have him and *he* begins to say he won't have *her—*

BENNET. Then it seems entirely settled on both sides. What am I supposed to do?

MRS. BENNET. *(Between sobs)* Tell her you insist on her marrying him. Elizabeth!

BENNET. Where *is* this misguided girl?

ELIZABETH. *(Who has just entered from library* R.*)* Here, sir.

BENNET. *(Looks at* MRS. BENNET. MRS. BENNET *nods directly. Sternly)* Come here, my child. (ELIZABETH *comes down and stands in front of him.* MRS. BENNET *crosses and stands behind* ELIZABETH.*)* I understand that Mr. Collins has made you an offer and that you have refused it.

ELIZABETH. I have, Papa.

BENNET. Very well, let's come to the point. Your mother insists on your accepting him. Isn't that so, Mrs. Bennet?

MRS. BENNET. Or else I shall never speak to her again.

BENNET. Then it seems that an unhappy alternative awaits you, Lizzie. *(Balances his glasses in his hand)* From this day forth you must be a stranger to one of your parents. Your mother will never speak to you again if you do *not* marry Mr. Collins— and I—will never speak to you again if you *do*.

ELIZABETH. Papa! *(Hugs him.* MRS. BENNET *sobs and sinks into sofa.)*

LYDIA. *(Enters through French windows; looks surprised at the hilarity, in which, of course,* MRS. BENNET *is definitely not sharing)* Well, thank heaven we're rid of Collins for the day. (EVERY-ONE *stares at her in surprise.)*

MRS. BENNET. *What?* Where—

LYDIA. *(Slyly)* He's just ridden off to the Lucases. He can't be back for hours.

MRS. BENNET. *(Gives a wail of despair)* Now see what you've done, Lizzie, you ungrateful girl! You've lost him, and that plainfaced scheming little cat will get him and turn us all out of here when your father dies.

ELIZABETH. Nonsense! Charlotte wouldn't look at him!

LYDIA. Not so hasty, Lizzie! Charlotte can't afford to be as particular as you—and she knows it.

MRS. BENNET. *(Wailing)* Lizzie, how can you decide to be an old maid? What a family I have! Lydia, why didn't you stop him? He might have had you.

BENNET. *(Going toward door* R.C.*)* Rubbish— Lizzie will be no old maid. Grant men a little judg- ment, my dear. The ineffable Collins is not the only example of his sex—thank God! *(Sends a smile to- ward his favorite,* ELIZABETH, *as he exits* R.C. *to* L.*)*

*(*JANE *enters from the library,* R.*; crosses to* MRS. BENNET.*)*

MRS. BENNET. Jane, dear!

JANE. *(Trying to smile)* Yes, Mama, did you want me?

MRS. BENNET. Oh, Jane, Lizzie is done for—she's going to be an old maid! *(Peers at* JANE*)* You've been crying. Oh, don't tell me that anything has

gone wrong between you and Mr. Bingley? Oh! Oh!
(ELIZABETH *crosses to* JANE; *puts her arm around
her.*)

LYDIA. (L. *of table* C.) Ha, ha, ha—we seem to
be the three graces nobody wants.

ELIZABETH. *(Fiercely)* Lydia! *(To* MRS. BEN-
NET*)* It's nothing, Mama. Jane had a letter from
Caroline Bingley—from London—

MRS. BENNET. *London!* You don't mean they have
left Netherfield?

JANE. *(Droops her head)* They've only gone up
to see some of the playhouses, Mama. I'm sure they'll
be back.

MRS. BENNET. I think Mr. Bingley should have
made an offer for you to your father before going
to London—he has compromised you enough with his
attentions—

JANE. Don't, Mama! *(She cannot control her
tears and breaks down.* ELIZABETH *takes her in her
arms.)*

MRS. BENNET. *(Looks at her a moment, then evidently gets a sudden idea)* I'll get Mr. Bennet. *(Exits
R.C. to L.* ELIZABETH *motions* LYDIA *to leave, across*
JANE's *bowed head.* LYDIA *gives a shrug; exits* R.C.
to L.)

ELIZABETH. *(Taking* JANE *to sofa)* Don't—darling—he'll come back. (BOTH *sit.)*

JANE. *(Through her tears)* But, Lizzie, he hasn't
sent one word—not one! I can't understand it. Caroline merely tells me they are not coming back until
the Spring—

ELIZABETH. Nonsense. You'll see, he will be here
to see Papa before the week is out. Only, darling,
don't trust Caroline Bingley. She's fond of you, I
know—but she doesn't want you as her brother's
wife.

JANE. Oh, no, Lizzie, Caroline has been so sweet
to me. She is incapable of deceit!

ELIZABETH. *(Tenderly)* All right, my sweet; believe in her as you do everyone. One comfort—even *she* can't persuade Charles that he doesn't love you.

JANE. *(After a pause)* But how can I marry him if his sister is against it?

ELIZABETH. *That* you must decide for yourself, my dearest little saint. If—you decide that the anguish of disobliging his cat of a sister is more than equal to the joy of marrying him—then I advise you to refuse him.

JANE. *(Laughing through her tears)* You naughty girl, Lizzie. You know very well that I should marry him if it vexed every relative he has. But if he doesn't come back—Lizzie, Lizzie—I couldn't bear it. *(Wistfully)* I think I should die.

ELIZABETH. He must come back—he won't be able not to— (BOTH *look toward door as* MRS. BENNET *re-enters* R.C. *from* L.)   *(WARN Curtain.)*

MRS. BENNET. *(At table* C.*)* Jane, dear, your father and I have decided to let you accept your Aunt Gardiner's invitation—to spend a few months with her and my brother in London.

JANE. *(Rises; goes to* MRS. BENNET—*overjoyed and astonished)* But, Mama—I didn't know my aunt had invited me—

MRS. BENNET. *(As diplomatically as she is able)* Never mind about that, my love. My letter will be on the way to London tomorrow, and your father is willing to take you up there as soon as you can make ready.

JANE. *(Seizes her mother and hugs her)* Mama!

ELIZABETH. *(Rises, looking at her mother in unaccustomed admiration and nodding)* Well, Mrs. Bennet—*you* certainly don't believe that marriages are made in Heaven—

MRS. BENNET. *(Sitting. Dryly)* From what I know of men, my dear—if we left it to them and Heaven—we should all be old maids!

ELIZABETH. *(Rushes to* MRS. BENNET*)* Mama—
(Kneels. As ELIZABETH *starts down—)*

CURTAIN

ACT TWO

SCENE II

SCENE: AUNT GARDINER'S *home at Cheapside, London. A month later; early spring afternoon.*

The room is small, simple, but bright and cheerful. Up Centre is a large curved bay window looking out over a garden. Against the window to the Right, a small love seat. Right of that a comfortable chair. Left Centre, also in the bow of the window, a gate-leg table set for tea—a large elaborate tea. Left of the table, another chair. A flower stand up Centre.

There is a door in the Right wall leading to the front portions of the house, and a door Left leading to the pantry or kitchen.

AT RISE: MRS. GARDINER *discovered* R. MAGGIE *enters* L. *with tea tray; places it on table.*

MAGGIE. Isn't it grand, ma'am, to see Miss Jane out at last? 'Tis lovely she looked going for her walk.

MRS. GARDINER. I hope Mary takes good care of her— *(Anxiously)* I do so want the dear child to have nice pink cheeks today—

MAGGIE. 'Tis wild she is about the tay party, ma'am. Do you like the way I've laid it?

MRS. GARDINER. *(Crosses to table. Examining table)* Oh, but Maggie—why only three cups?

MAGGIE. Blessed be to God, ma'am—I thought only the grand Miss Bingley was afther comin'.

MRS. GARDINER. *(Smiling)* Miss Bingley has a brother, Maggie.

MAGGIE. Oh, ma'am dear—do ye mane it? Himself is comin' too?

MRS. GARDINER. *(Smiling)* Wait and see. In the meantime, bring another cup and saucer—and remember, everything must be perfect for Miss Jane's sake. This is a great day for her.

MAGGIE. Rely on me, ma'am— I'd lay down and die for Miss Jane—

MRS. GARDINER. We must show Miss Bingley that we may not be as grand as she but we are just as genteel even though we do live in Cheapside.

JANE. *(Enters* R. *with a letter in her hand.* MAGGIE *exits* L.*)* Auntie, I've had such a lovely walk—I feel almost well again now—

MRS. GARDINER. *(Crosses to* JANE*)* After Miss Bingley's visit, I am sure you will feel better still— Eh, darling? *(Smiles.)*

JANE. And wait till I tell you the news about Lizzie. *(Sets parasol.)*

MRS. GARDINER. *(Remembering suddenly)* What, you've had a letter from her?

JANE. *(Chuckling)* Yes! What do you think, Auntie—she's actually staying at Rosings—with Lady Catherine de Bourgh—she was invited with Mr. and Mrs. Collins!

MRS. GARDINER. Mrs. Collins? *(Astounded)* But I thought that silly young man had made an offer to Lizzie.

JANE. Yes—and after she rejected him he tried Charlotte Lucas—with better result— *(Laughs)* Mama has refused to kiss Lizzie good-night ever since.

MRS. GARDINER. *(Crosses to table; arranges*

flowers) I should think Mrs. Bennet would have thanked heaven instead.

JANE. Oh, no. Mama regards any husband as better than no husband. *(Taking off coat, places it on sofa. Demurely)* Only Papa and Lizzie happen to think differently. *(Pauses)* About marriage, Mama is not very romantic. *(Sits on sofa.)*

MRS. GARDINER. That is the most penetrating observation I have ever heard from your innocent lips, Jane. *(Laughs.)*

JANE. I wonder how Lizzie will like Lady Catherine de Bourgh? I hear she is even more imposing than Mr. Darcy. He is at Rosings, too. Lizzie detests him but I have always liked him. I feel that under that proud shy manner he is—

MRS. GARDINER. *(Interrupting. Crosses to C.)* You like all the world, darling, bless your sweet heart!

MAGGIE. *(Enters L. with teacup, which she sets on table)* Sure, ma'am, 'tis herself that's driving up to the front door now in the grandest carriage. Miss Bingley, ma'am, it must be, for I never see the like of the two horses and the coachmen.

JANE. Is Miss Bingley alone, Maggie?

MAGGIE. I couldn't see plainly, but 'tis sure I am himself must be sittin' in the carriage beside her.

MRS. GARDINER. Hurry, Maggie. Go and open the door! *(To JANE as MAGGIE exits R. Wishing to leave her alone to greet the BINGLEYS. Kisses her tenderly)* Thank goodness you look so bright. Well, Jane— *(Takes JANE'S things)* I'll take your things and go and see that the scones are hot— *(Exits R. JANE, trembling, watches R. door. Rises. Expecting CHARLES and CAROLINE.)*

MAGGIE. *(Enters R.; announces. MAGGIE'S face is sad; her voice pitched unconsciously lower)* Miss Bingley— *(Exits L.)*

MISS BINGLEY. *(Enters R. Quite aware of JANE'S*

shocked look) Jane, dear, I have been pining to see you.

JANE. Dear Caroline. I'm very happy to see you again. (MISS BINGLEY *sits in chair* R. *of sofa.)* Is everyone well—? Mr. Darcy? Your brother? *(She sits.)*

MISS BINGLEY. Oh, very well indeed, my dear. We have all be so busy. Miss Georgiana Darcy is up in town for her first season, you know. She and her brother have been entertaining vastly at the Darcy house.

JANE. Mr. Darcy is quite devoted to his sister, isn't he?

MISS BINGLEY. *(Archly)* He is not the only one. Indeed, she is so lovely one can't wonder—and all that fortune. Why, do you know, she will have twenty thousand pounds when she is of age. Quite a breath-taking sum, isn't it? Not that money matters to either Charles or myself—still, one can't have too much of it.

JANE. *(Starts, but instantly recovers herself)* But I am sure that with such a sweet girl as Miss Darcy, money counts very little. She has many suitors, I suppose— *(Wistfully—still unsuspecting.)*

MISS BINGLEY. Naturally—but you can be sure that the Darcy family will only allow her to take a young gentleman of the highest connections. *(Pauses)* You don't look as well as you did in the country, my dear. Have you been poorly?

JANE. Oh, no—I have never felt better. I am always a little pale in the city; I miss the fresh air.

MISS BINGLEY. Oh! *(Pause.)*

JANE. Are you—and your brother staying much longer in London, Caroline—?

MISS BINGLEY. Only until the conclusion of this affair.

JANE. *(Looks mystified, then frightened, then controls herself)* Some business, Caroline?

MISS BINGLEY. *(In an affectedly confidential tone)*
I wouldn't confide this to anyone else—but you and
I are such close friends—even though I have had no
time at all to give myself the pleasure of visiting you
here—you promise to keep it a secret?

JANE. Of course!

MISS BINGLEY. *(Leaning forward; in a low tone)*
I am hoping to hear the happy news any day now. I
know you will be the first to wish them joy—

JANE. *(Faintly)* Them? Joy?

MISS BINGLEY. Charles—and dear Georgiana—

JANE. *(Softly)* Indeed, indeed, I wish them joy
—if they truly love each other.

MISS BINGLEY. *(Sentimentally)* Oh, the dear boy
is so much in love— I tease him all the time. He is
never home now—escorting Miss Darcy here, there,
everywhere—balls, routs, the playhouse. Mr. Darcy
and I have wanted this match for ever so long. Thank
you for your wishes. I'll convey them to Charles!

(MRS. GARDINER *enters* R.)

JANE. *(Making an effort. Rises)* Miss Bingley,
may I present my aunt, Mrs. Gardiner?

MRS. GARDINER. Permit me to welcome you, Miss
Bingley.

MISS BINGLEY. *(Simultaneously with* MRS. GAR-
DINER*)* I'm vastly pleased, ma'am. Oh, I forgot in
all my excitement—Charles sends you his best respects.

JANE. Thank him for me. (MAGGIE *enters* L. *with
tea and scones on tray; sets it on table up* L.)

MRS. GARDINER. *(Crosses to table and begins pouring tea)* May I offer you some tea, Miss Bingley?

MISS BINGLEY. *(Sitting)* Thank you, just the
tiniest cup—

MRS. GARDINER. *(Pouring tea)* Sugar? And milk,
Miss Bingley?

MISS BINGLEY. No, thank you.

JANE. It is so sweet of you to find time to visit my aunt, dear Caroline.

MISS BINGLEY. I should have been here earlier, only I have been really persecuted with invitations. (MAGGIE *serves* MISS BINGLEY.)

MRS. GARDINER. Jane, dearest, I've made your tea stronger. *(Hands cup to* MAGGIE, *who serves it to* JANE) Jane is over-tired—gadding about so much since she came to London.

MISS BINGLEY. But I didn't know you had any acquaintances here— *(Astonished.)*

MRS. GARDINER. *(Quietly)* Is that why you have been so attentive to her?

MISS BINGLEY. *(Embarrassed)* I didn't know she had come to London until she called—

MRS. GARDINER. Nearly a month ago.

JANE. *Auntie,* I have no claim on Miss Bingley's time. She has many friends in London of much longer standing.

MISS BINGLEY. *(Rising.* JANE *and* MRS. GARDINER *rise.)* Indeed, dear Jane, you understand perfectly. (MAGGIE *crosses and takes* MISS BINGLEY's *cup and takes it back to table* L. *To* MRS. GARDINER) She is always so sweet about one's difficulties— (MRS. GARDINER *bows gravely.)* Even this short visit has simply bankrupted my time. Mr. Darcy's visiting his aunt at Rosings means that I have to take Miss Georgiana entirely under my wing until his return. *(Simpering. To* MRS. GARDINER) I can't leave those two young people alone, you know—the betrothal is not announced yet. It has been so nice to meet you, Mrs. Gardiner—   *(WARN Curtain.)*

MRS. GARDINER. Attend Miss Bingley to her coach, Maggie. (MAGGIE *crosses and exits* R.)

MISS BINGLEY. Goodbye, dear Jane. It has been a delight to see you again. *(Kisses* JANE's *cheek)* Good afternoon, ma'am. *(To* MRS. GARDINER, *who returns her curtsey.* MISS BINGLEY *exits* R.)

JANE. Oh, Auntie! *(Turns to* MRS. GARDINER, *crying.)*

MRS. GARDINER. *(Crosses to* JANE; *embraces her)* There, there, my darling, I know— It's the disillusionment that cuts the very heart—

JANE. *(Weeping)* But to abandon me—without a word! What could I have done to him? He loved me, Auntie—he did, he did! *(Low)* He *kissed* me once—and— *(Shamefacedly)* I kissed him. *(Looks anxiously into her aunt's face)* You believe—don't you—that I should never have done *that* if I hadn't been sure he wanted to make me an offer—don't you, Auntie?

MRS. GARDINER. Of course I do, my lamb! *(She sits on sofa, holding on to* JANE'S *hands.)*

JANE. And do you suppose *he* understands that too? I wouldn't have him think ill of me.

MRS. GARDINER. It's all a mystery to me— *(Reflects, puzzled)* When I met him at Longbourn he seemed such a properly sweet young gentleman—

JANE. *(Kneels)* Oh, he *is*— I do assure you, Auntie—he *is*—and now it's all over— I can't bear it; I can't, I can't— *(Bursts into low, broken sobs. During this speech* JANE *sinks upon the floor beside* MRS. GARDINER. *Breaks into sobs, her head in* MRS. GARDINER'S *lap.)*

CURTAIN

SCENE III

SCENE: LADY CATHERINE DE BOURGH'S *drawing room at Rosings Park, Hunsford, Kent. Morning.*

A Regency drawing room with deep Empire-green walls and white woodwork. There is an

*ancestral portrait over the mantel Centre, flanked
by two white doors piercing the deep green of
the walls. These doors are not used.*

*The SUNLIGHT pours in through the open
windows Right, looking on gardens and an ex-
panse of lawn.*

*A chair up Right; tables Right and Left of
mantel; seat in front of mantel; chair up Left;
circular tables with chairs Right Centre and Left
Centre.*

AT RISE: ELIZABETH *is sitting in chair* R. *of table*
L.C., *writing letter.*

DARCY. *(Enters* L. *Closes doors. She looks up at
him and smiles. He crosses to her, but slows up a
bit as she turns back to the letter)* Good morning,
Miss Elizabeth.

ELIZABETH. Good morning! *(Looks at him a moment, then resumes writing.)*

DARCY. It seems a pity to be wasting all this sunshine.

ELIZABETH. *(Continuing her writing)* It would
be if one were doing so without good reason.

DARCY. *(Crosses toward her)* You are writing
letters?

ELIZABETH. Shall we say I was trying to?

DARCY. Pray do not let me disturb you.

ELIZABETH. *(Very coldly)* Was there something
you wished to say, Mr. Darcy?

DARCY. *(Crosses to French windows; looks out.
Longing to remain, so hopeful to start a conversation,
turns to her)* I was wondering whether you were
pleased with Kent?

ELIZABETH. I prefer Hertfordshire.

DARCY. *(Trying again)* We have had little opportunity for conversing these past two days. I was
surprised to discover you a fellow guest at my aunt's.
(She smiles acquiescent.)

ELIZABETH. I too was surprised. I had expected to visit the Collins' at the parsonage. I was not prepared for such an excess of hospitality on the part of your aunt.

DARCY. She likes to have young people about her. But I did not know you were to be here.

ELIZABETH. *(Willfully misunderstanding)* Otherwise you might have remained in town?

DARCY. *(Quietly)* On the contrary; I should have come with even greater alacrity. *(He bows.)*

ELIZABETH. You surprise me, sir; I did not know you were so sociably inclined.

DARCY. Usually I am not. *(She dips her pen into inkwell; looks at the pen.)* You wish to continue writing. *(Crosses to chair* R. *of* R.C. *table)* But when you have more leisure.

ELIZABETH. Mr. Darcy, if it is conversation you are in need of, I am sure your aunt, Lady Catherine, will be delighted to furnish it. You must excuse me. I have to finish my letter.

COLLINS. *(Enters* L.*)* Cousin, Cousin, you are surely not aware that Her Ladyship has been asking for you? She intends to join you presently.

ELIZABETH. I am honored, but I am very busy, Mr. Collins.

COLLINS. Busy! No one is busy when Lady Catherine de Bourgh honors them with her attention.

DARCY. It would seem that you have discovered an exception, Mr. Collins.

COLLINS. You must forgive my cousin; she has had so few advantages— *(He fusses about fixing a chair for* LADY CATHERINE*)* I like to prepare things for Lady Catherine. She is accustomed to deference. Ah, Her Ladyship is coming— Are you certain you're quite ready, Cousin?

ELIZABETH. *(Twiddles her thumbs)* Yes, Mr. Collins.

(LADY CATHERINE *sweeps in from* L. ELIZABETH
    crosses to R. *of table and curtseys.* DARCY *bows.*
    COLLINS *stands behind* LADY CATHERINE, *who
    crosses in front of table* L.C. *to* C.)

LADY CATHERINE. Ah, here you are, Darcy! It is
kind of you to amuse Miss Bennet until I can enter-
tain her. Miss Bennet, I was sorry to notice your
small appetite at breakfast. It is not a sensible habit
to make a light meal in the morning. Oh, that window so widely open. The sunlight is very bad for
really good furniture. (COLLINS *hurries over to window to close it.)* No, no, Collins, leave it alone.
Where is Fitzwilliam?

DARCY. Still asleep, I believe.

LADY CATHERINE. Asleep? And it's close on to
nine o'clock. Whatever can he be thinking of?

DARCY. Of nothing, I should judge. Remember,
he has been fighting for his country in India. He
has a right to be somewhat tired.

LADY CATHERINE. He has no right to be late for
breakfast in my house. (LADY CATHERINE *crosses to
table* R.C.) What were you and Miss Bennet saying
to each other, Darcy? Ah, you are writing letters, I
see, Miss Bennet. *(She looks at the letter on* ELIZA-
BETH'S *pad.)*

ELIZABETH. I was. (DARCY *crosses up.* ELIZA-
BETH *closes her writing case as if by accident.)*

LADY CATHERINE. But why in this room? We
always write our letters in the library.

ELIZABETH. Yes, I know, Lady Catherine— But
the library does not possess such a view—and I write
with so much more inspiration when looking out on
green trees and flowers. *(Goes to window; looks
out.* DARCY *crosses to back of table.)* Look at that
hawthorne hedge over there. (LADY CATHERINE
crosses to window to look out.)

COLLINS. But you have not seen half the beauty

of Rosings yet, Cousin. That view is trifling—merely trifling!

LADY CATHERINE. That, Miss Bennet, is not a view at all. *(To* COLLINS*)* Miss Bennet has only been here two days, and most of that time has been spent in Fitzwilliam's company, Mr. Collins. My estate would require a month at least to appreciate all its varied prospects. *(Crosses to chair* R. *of* L.C. *table. Looks around to see why* COLLINS *hasn't placed chair for her)* Collins! (COLLINS *does so quickly.)*

DARCY. *(Coming down to* LADY CATHERINE*)* I believe Miss Bennet wishes to finish her letter, Aunt.

LADY CATHERINE. Nonsense, Darcy! (DARCY *crosses to table* L.C.) I haven't had sufficient leisure to become acquainted with Miss Bennet since her arrival. It's fortunate that I happen to have a little time this morning. We are waiting for Mrs. Collins to accompany us on our weekly duty visits to the cottagers. Now, my child. *(Points to chair* L. *of* L.C. *table.* ELIZABETH *sits there.)* You did not finish telling me about your sisters last evening. How many did you say you had?

ELIZABETH. Two, your Ladyship.

LADY CATHERINE. And how many carriages does your papa keep, my dear? (DARCY *crosses to* R. *of fireplace.)*

ELIZABETH. One, Lady Catherine. (LADY CATHERINE *looks at her pityingly.* ELIZABETH *looks at* COLLINS, *who is very upset.)*

LADY CATHERINE. What was your mama's maiden name?

ELIZABETH. *(Mischievously)* Gardiner, ma'am, and she has a brother who lives in Cheapside. He's an attorney, and—

COLLINS. Oh, Cousin, I beg of you!

LADY CATHERINE. Never mind, Collins, I choose not to have heard. *(She pauses a moment)* Do you play, my child, and sing?

ELIZABETH. A little.

LADY CATHERINE. I am happy to hear it. Music is, of all subjects, my delight. I should have been a great proficient if I had learned.

COLLINS. Oh, I am sure you would, Lady Catherine!

LADY CATHERINE. Has your governess left you?

ELIZABETH. We never had a governess— (COLLINS *looks crestfallen at the shame of his relatives.*)

LADY CATHERINE. *What? No governess!* Great Heavens! I have never heard of such a thing. Your mama must have been a perfect slave to your education.

ELIZABETH. Oh, no!

LADY CATHERINE. *(Lorgnettes* ELIZABETH*)* Pray what is your age?

ELIZABETH. As I am still unmarried, Your Ladyship can hardly expect me to answer that question.

LADY CATHERINE. You can't be more than twenty, so there is plenty of time before you need begin lying about your age. (DARCY *crosses up to* R.) If you receive no offer before you are thirty, why, then—

ELIZABETH. *(Sweetly)* Is there anything else you would like to know about me, Lady Catherine?

LADY CATHERINE. Well, my dear, I think you've told us enough about yourself for this morning. *(Kindly)* We can hear the rest another time— Now I really must devote some of my attention to Mrs. Collins. (DARCY *crosses the French windows.*) Collins, hurry her— (COLLINS *bows.* ELIZABETH *rises to behind table* L.C. FITZWILLIAM *enters* L. *and bows to* COLLINS *stiffly, who exits* L.)

FITZWILLIAM. Good morning, Aunt. Good morning, Miss Elizabeth.

ELIZABETH. Good morning, sir.

FITZWILLIAM. Ah, Darcy—

LADY CATHERINE. Fitzwilliam, I fully appreciate all that you have done for England, but you're expected to appear in time for breakfast here, do you understand?

FITZWILLIAM. *(Thoroughly apologetic)* Forgive me. *(Takes her hand and kisses it)* I overslept. I am a lazy beggar, you know—and take every advantage of such a charming hostess— *(He bows to* LADY CATHERINE.*)*

LADY CATHERINE. Tut, tut—you are incorrigible. Miss Bennet will receive a false impression of your habits.

ELIZABETH. On the contrary, Lady Catherine, I have already received only the best. *(Smiles at* FITZWILLIAM.*)*

FITZWILLIAM. 'Pon my honor. You know, that is quite a spontaneous compliment. Dashed if it isn't. I hope I shan't disappoint you. *(To* DARCY*)* Did you hear that, Darcy?

DARCY. And Miss Bennet is not easily impressed, Aunt.

ELIZABETH. *(To* LADY CATHERINE*)* You see how unfortunate I am in meeting with a gentleman so well able to expose my real character, Lady Catherine. (LADY CATHERINE *stares at her.*) And in a part of the world when I had hoped to pass myself off with some degree of credit—

DARCY. *(Puzzled)* But I have said nothing to your discredit, Miss Bennet—there could be nothing to say—

LADY CATHERINE. I do not understand your meaning, Miss Bennet— My nephew is too gentlemanlike to expose anybody—

FITZWILLIAM. *(Chuckling)* Pray, Miss Elizabeth— *(Crossing to* ELIZABETH, *takes her arm.* BOTH *cross in front of seat up* C.*)* I should like to hear something about Darcy. Why don't you retaliate and expose *him?* How did he behave in Hertfordshire society?

ELIZABETH. Very strangely!

LADY CATHERINE. Miss Bennet!

ELIZABETH. I am sorry, ma'am, but truth compels me to state that he was unsociable and silent most of the time.

DARCY. I lack the talent for conversing easily with strangers.

ELIZABETH. And those who are beneath your dignity are all strangers. And must forever remain strangers. Is that not so, Mr. Darcy?

DARCY. I find myself unable to provide an answer, Miss Bennet. *(He gives her a look and turns; bows stiffly.* ELIZABETH *curtseys primly and* DARCY *exits at windows.)*

LADY CATHERINE. Were you criticizing my nephew, Miss Bennet?

ELIZABETH. Criticizing Mr. Darcy? Oh, Lady Catherine!

LADY CATHERINE. No, I thought you would not presume to. (COLLINS *enters* L. *with* CHARLOTTE, *crossing to* L. *of* LADY CATHERINE. CHARLOTTE *down stage.* FITZWILLIAM *stands* L. *of sofa.)* He has misunderstood you.

FITZWILLIAM. Ah, Mrs. Collins, good morning.

ELIZABETH. Charl!

LADY CATHERINE. Oh, Mrs. Collins, you must have forgotten how I dislike to be kept waiting.

COLLINS. Mrs. Collins was gathering together the accounts Your Ladyship so graciously asked for. *(Crosses behind* LADY CATHERINE.*)*

LADY CATHERINE. Ah, yes, the accounts for the feed of your poultry and cows, Mrs. Collins.

CHARLOTTE. *(Crosses to* L. *of* LADY CATHERINE; *hands her the bills)* Yes, Your Ladyship—I had to send one of your footmen to the parsonage for the latest one—they are all there. *(Turns to* ELIZABETH*)* You see how fortunate I am, Lizzie.

ELIZABETH. Yes, I am beginning to, Charlotte dear. (COLLINS *smiles at* ELIZABETH.)

CHARLOTTE. *(In the same tone)* Nothing is too

insignificant for Her Ladyship's kind attention. (COL-
LINS *beams*. LADY CATHERINE *glows.*) —even in
such a small household as mine—

COLLINS. *(Reprovingly) Ours,* my love!

LADY CATHERINE. Indeed, my dear—'tis the least
I can do—

FITZWILLIAM. I say!

ELIZABETH. Oh, Charlotte! *(Rises;*
steps down R. COLLINS *crosses down* *(Together.)*
to R. *of table.)*

LADY CATHERINE. *(Rises)* But come now—we
must set out— *(To* COLLINS*)* I have heard that
some of the cottagers are disposed to be quarrelsome
again—

COLLINS. I have told them so often the duty of
counting their blessings, Your Ladyship—

CHARLOTTE. You wouldn't believe, *Lizzie,* how dis-
contented some of those foolish people are with their
nice little two-roomed cottages— But Lady Catherine settles all their differences and silences their complaints.

ELIZABETH. *(Dryly)* I can well imagine it.

LADY CATHERINE. Now I will really listen to no
more compliments for today, my dears. Come, Mrs.
Collins. We must go to your parsonage first. You
and Mr. Collins may walk across— *(Leads* CHAR-
LOTTE *toward window)* —and I will drive over in
the phaeton and join you. *(She turns to* ELIZABETH*)*
Good morning, Miss Bennet. Are you coming, Fitzwilliam? (ELIZABETH *curtseys and exchanges glances*
with CHARLOTTE.)

FITZWILLIAM. No, thank you, Aunt. I don't feel
as well qualified as you and Mr. Collins to tell the
villagers how to live.

LADY CATHERINE. You are probably right.

FITZWILLIAM. I shall stay and plague Miss Bennet
a little longer, and then find Darcy and go for my
constitutional. *(Laughs.)*

LADY CATHERINE. Very well— *(Crosses to front of* R.C. *table. To* ELIZABETH*)* Oh, and remind me, my child— (ELIZABETH *crosses to back of table.)* Before you seal your letter, I want to send some advice to your mother. I will speak to you later about it. Come, my dears— *(She exits French windows.* COLLINS *raises her umbrella and hurries out, holding it over her.* CHARLOTTE *raises her umbrella and sends a backward look at* ELIZABETH *and follows them out.)*

ELIZABETH. *(Crosses to windows)* Oh, my poor Charlotte!

FITZWILLIAM. *(Crosses to her)* Come, now, cheer up. Why don't you come for a walk with me? You can write your dashed old letter later—

ELIZABETH. It is tempting out there—in that dewdrenched world—it's all so green and wet and shining. No, I shall be firm— *(At chair* R. *of* L.C. *table)* I will meet you on your way back, though I shall have to do it by stealth.

FITZWILLIAM. Good! By jove, it must be dull being a girl. *(Crosses to table)* I have often thought about it—never going anywhere alone—sitting knitting or netting—whatever it is you call it—purses and things—waiting for some chap to make you an offer— Egad! How does a girl like you put up with it?

ELIZABETH. Well, for one thing, I don't net purses and I am not waiting for any offers and I actually came to Hunsford alone in the mail coach. Now what do you think of that?

FITZWILLIAM. *(Crosses to* R. *of her)* You are too intelligent for a young lady—that's your trouble.

ELIZABETH. And for most of the young gentlemen I meet— *(He stands awkwardly. She crosses to* L. *of* L.C. *table)* And now, Colonel, what about your constitutional and my letter?

FITZWILLIAM. I say, Miss Elizabeth— Do you mind if I ask you something?

ELIZABETH. *(Sits* L. *of* L.C. *table)* As long as I don't have to answer—

FITZWILLIAM. *(Sits* R. *of table, facing* ELIZABETH*)* It's about Darcy— You hurt him just now— I'm fond of the solemn old owl— Why are you so prejudiced against him?

ELIZABETH. Prejudiced? I didn't know I was that. Frankly, I dislike him. It isn't very polite to show it—I hoped I did not. I have very good reasons for my—prejudice—as to that— You might ask him why he adopts such a superior attitude.

FITZWILIAM. It's that confounded pride of his. It is always mistaken for conceit. But when you really know him, he's—

ELIZABETH. Is there really much to know beyond a supreme self-assurance and a disdain for anyone under a peer? Such snobbery in a well-born man is incomprehensible to me. I always thought only inferior people were snobs.

FITZWILLIAM. Well, it's surprising how many well-born people are like that—it's taught them by nursemaids and governesses when they are youngsters—but Darcy has an awfully decent character underneath all that nonsense. He has a heart and a mind too, if you can only get him to open up—

ELIZABETH. I shouldn't bother to try—

FITZWILLIAM. I'd really like to change your opinion about the old sobersides—I'm such a stupid ass, I have no vocabulary when I want to convince.

ELIZABETH. You're a loyal friend, and I like you for it—but I am wondering, nevertheless, if you could really mention *one* kind of action—

FITZWILLIAM. *(Rising; standing above chair; interrupting her)* Yes, I can tell you one—

ELIZABETH. *(With a pretty air of being judicial)* Let me hear it.

FITZWILLIAM. Very well. What would you say if I told you that he stayed tied to London all last winter—just to keep a friend away from temptation?

ELIZABETH. Temptation?

FITZWILLIAM. The temptation of   king a disastrous marriage.

ELIZABETH. Oh!

FITZWILLIAM. This friend of   s—chap named Dingley or Bingley or something l ke that—evidently conceived a consuming passion for a designing minx he met at some outlandish place in the country.

ELIZABETH. That happens so often, doesn't it?

FITZWILLIAM. Yes, doesn't it! Of course, she cared nothing for *him.* *(Looks at him.)* Only wanted his name and his fortune. She was aided in her nefarious schemes by a particularly awful specimen of a mother.

ELIZABETH. Perhaps it was one of those mothers whose kind intentions are often fatal to those she most wishes to help.

FITZWILLIAM. Probably. But in addition to that, the girl had a pair of sisters who must have been veritable she-wolves. Poor Bingley was as good as caught. *(Crosses to table* R.C.)

ELIZABETH. *(Rises, turning to him)* But Darcy snatched him from the jaws of the she-wolves? *(Crosses up to fireplace.)*

FITZWILLIAM. Exactly. Oh—he only mentioned it to me because I happened to ask him why he'd stayed so unusually long in town. It was really a frightfully decent, unselfish thing for him to have done.

ELIZABETH. Indeed it was! And I see I have been underrating Mr. Darcy. I did not know he was made of such heroic stuff.

FITZWILLIAM. *(Uneasily)* Yes—rather! I say, Miss Bennet, are you laughing at me?

ELIZABETH. Oh, no, Colonel, not at *you!* *(Crosses to chair* L. *of table* R.C.)

FITZWILLIAM. I did want you to know the truth!

DARCY. *(Entering* R.*)* Oh, Fitzwilliam, are you going out?

FITZWILLIAM. I was, but I'll wait.

DARCY. No, no— If you will take the same road as we discovered yesterday, I will join you a little later.

FITZWILLIAM. Good. Au revoir, Miss Bennet— *(He bows; exits quickly* R. ELIZABETH *sits chair* R. *of* L.C. *table.)*

DARCY. Miss Elizabeth—I wish to speak to you.

ELIZABETH. I should have thought it evident that I wished to finish my letter.

DARCY. You're not very polite. You were such a stickler for politeness in Hertfordshire. *(He smiles.)*

ELIZABETH. We are most of us sticklers for virtues in other people. *(Continues writing.)*

DARCY. *(Moves to table)* Miss Elizabeth—

ELIZABETH. *(Looks up and stops writing)* Sir? *(He moves away* C. *She looks after him. He turns.)* What *is* it, Mr. Darcy?

DARCY. *(Paces up and down; suddenly crosses to* R. *of* ELIZABETH*)* It's no use— In vain have I struggled; my feelings will not be repressed. You must allow me to tell you how ardently I admire and love you. *(She rises.)* I've fought with myself all these months— (ELIZABETH *stares at him, too stunned to speak.)* You may think I am speaking without due thought—that my feeling for you outweighs my common sense—that this love for you that consumes me is a thing that will pass. But it is not so, Miss Elizabeth. I have learned that in the bitterness of my self-abasement. *(Pause)* I love you.

ELIZABETH. Do you expect me to take you seriously? Have you so quickly forgotten the inferiority of my family?

DARCY. I have forgotten nothing about you—I love you.

ELIZABETH. Have you considered my unsuitability in the eyes of your exalted world, Mr. Darcy?

DARCY. I have considered it—and I love you.

ELIZABETH. *(Angrily)* You need not say it again, sir! What am I supposed to reply to this extraordinary harangue? One can scarcely call it an offer of marriage. You do not, I suppose, expect me to feel flattered?

DARCY. But do you expect me to be glad that your family is inferior to mine? Or blame me for being honest and sincere when making the most momentous decision of my life?

ELIZABETH. Decision—?

DARCY. Yes, my dearest. I have decided to ask you to marry me.

ELIZABETH. *(Facing him)* I suppose I should be overwhelmed at this honor.

DARCY. *(Drawing back)* But—

ELIZABETH. I ought to congratulate you on overcoming the battle between your unwilling affection and my unworthiness—but you see, I happen to be quite uninterested in your problems— *(Crosses down c.)*

DARCY. Elizabeth— *(He approaches her again, his hand out. She repels him with a proud gesture. He is about to speak.)*

ELIZABETH. *(Turns to him)* If you were not so lacking in perception, sir, you might have spared yourself my refusal—

DARCY. *(Dumbfounded. He crosses a step to her)* You refuse me?

ELIZABETH. *(Quietly)* You might have noticed the fact long ago. I have never hidden it. I neither aspire to nor could I ever return your affection. As for your scruples about marrying into my family—don't let that ever concern you again. *(Crosses to table L.C.)*

DARCY. Is that all the reply I am to be honored

with? I might perhaps deserve to be told why I have been rejected—and with so little civility.

ELIZABETH. I also might deserve to know why you consider my feelings so little while expressing your own.

DARCY. *(Takes step to her)* Please—if the manner of my revelation has offended you—

ELIZABETH. I am influenced by something deeper than your manners, Mr. Darcy. I am thinking more of your fine capacity for cruelty.

DARCY. Cruelty? And when have I demonstrated that capacity?

ELIZABETH. Mr. Darcy, have you never willfully injured an innocent person?

DARCY. *(After a moment of thought)* Oh, you are referring again to my treatment of Mr. Wickham? That still preys on you. The fascination inferior men exert over superior women has often been a puzzle to me.

ELIZABETH. Inferior! Do you always apply that word only to other people?

DARCY. I feel justified in using it towards Mr. Wickham—unless indeed the word "cad" might be more descriptive. If the principal evidence against me is based on your faith in the word of a man like him—

ELIZABETH. This is unworthy of you, sir.

DARCY. I know you don't choose to believe me, but let me most earnestly warn you against him. He is an unprincipled, designing—   *(WARN Curtain.)*

ELIZABETH. *(Turns head)* I refuse to listen to you any further, but it is not only what you have done to Mr. Wickham, although that would be quite enough— *(Faces DARCY)* Even if I cared for you, and I never could—nothing would induce me to marry the man who has ruined my sister's life. *(Her voice breaks)* The sweetest soul ever born! How could you do it? How could you have hurt her—

having once known her? ! (DARCY *is silent.)* Can you deny that you came between Jane and Charles Bingley?

DARCY. I did everything in my power to separate my friend from your sister. *(Quietly.* ELIZABETH *rises.)* Towards him I have been wiser than towards myself.

ELIZABETH. You talk to me of love— They love each other, she and Charles— Jane is of those who only love once. It will kill her, I know it will. *(Pause)* You have trodden on a heart.

DARCY. *(After a silence)* You wish to think badly of me.

ELIZABETH. *(Turns away from him)* I have no choice.

DARCY. I have made the mistake of being honest with you.

ELIZABETH. *(Turns to him)* Honesty is a very overrated virtue. Tact and taste are more agreeable ones.

DARCY. My scruples with regard to your family— were natural.

ELIZABETH. And should have been kept to yourself. Let us end this distasteful subject— *(Turns to* DARCY) You could not have made your offer in any way that would have tempted me to accept it. Mr. Darcy, you are the last man in the world whom I could ever be prevailed upon to marry!

DARCY. *(He is humiliated, shocked and astounded)* Forgive me for having taken up your time. *(He bows; crosses to door* L.) I wish you every happiness. *(Her face is slightly panicked as he begins to go.)*

CURTAIN

ACT THREE

Scene I

Scene: *The drawing room-living room at Long-bourn. Same as Act I. A week later. Afternoon.*
L. of R.C. doors closed in this scene. R. open. Serving table R. of the door.

At Rise: Mrs. Lake *and* Elizabeth *enter through conservatory.* Elizabeth *sighs.*

Mrs. Lake. Don't you worry about Miss Jane, Miss.

Elizabeth. I'm all right; I'm just tired, Mrs. Lake.

Mrs. Lake. You can't believe how glad I was to see you last night, Miss Elizabeth. The responsibility was too much for me.

Elizabeth. I came home as soon as I got Papa's message. Jane seems happier out there where she can see the flowers, doesn't she, Mrs. Lake? (Elizabeth *crosses slowly to front of table* c.)

Mrs. Lake. *(At chair* r. *of table* c.*)* Aye, the apothecary was right, Miss Bennet. (Elizabeth *crosses to sofa and sits.)* And it's no trouble for Hill and me to carry her downstairs every morning. *(Takes a step toward* Elizabeth) If I might take the liberty, Miss—couldn't we hint to the young gentleman—

ELIZABETH. Oh, no, no—she would never forgive us.

MRS. LAKE. If you'll excuse me, Miss, it would be best to keep Mrs. Bennet away from her as much as possible. It upsets Miss Jane to have your lady mother always blaming a Mr. Bingley—

ELIZABETH. *(Looks annoyed at the news of her mother's indiscretion)* Yes, I will tell Mama! You see, she is so anxious that she imagines all sorts of things—

(At MR. BENNET'S *entrance,* R.C. *from* L., MRS. LAKE *drops a respectful curtsey.* BENNET *bows to her.* MRS. LAKE *exits through the conservatory.)*

BENNET. *(Enters; crosses to* L. *end of sofa)* Lizzie, my dear, are you very tired? How is Jane? Was it a bad night? *(Sits on sofa.)*

ELIZABETH. Papa, I'm worried. She seems so languid. When I speak to her she just gives that angelic smile— *(Voice breaks)* You know it— Oh, Papa, what have they done to her? (ELIZABETH *lays her head on his shoulder.)*

BENNET. *(Comforting her)* Don't, Lizzie, my child! We can't have you losing courage— If there's no change by tomorrow I have decided to call a physician down from London. It's *you* I am worried about. You're not getting any sleep. There is too much on your shoulders— Your mother, as usual, is quite useless in a crisis.

MRS. BENNET. *(Enters* R.C. *from* L.; *stands just below the door)* I don't think that's a proper way to speak of your wife, Mr. Bennet. You should not blame me for my wretched nerves. (BENNET *crosses to fireplace* L.; *lights pipe.)* How is our poor Jane? I must see if she is warm enough out there.

ELIZABETH. *(Crosses to* MRS. BENNET*)* Please don't, Mama—don't disturb her. I promised Mrs.

Lake we would all keep away from her until she wakes up. (ELIZABETH *crosses back to sofa; sits at* R. *end of it.)*

MRS. BENNET. What a comfort to have you home again, Lizzie—with everything at sixes and sevens— *(Gets sewing from table* R. *of door* R.C.*)* —our darling Jane brought back unconscious. All the fault of that fickle Mr. Bingley.

BENNET. I hope you will have the sense to refrain from those observations in anyone else's company. They humiliate your daughter.

MRS. BENNET. *(Crosses to sofa and sits. Plaintively)* Well, if she dies of a broken heart, it will be a comfort to know that that young man is responsible.

BENNET. *(Crosses to sofa)* You certainly get your comfort in queer ways, Mrs. Bennet. *(To* ELIZABETH, *suddenly)* Lizzie, your Aunt Gardiner told us that Jane had not been well for some time in London—

ELIZABETH. Auntie should have let us know. I would have gone straight there. (ELIZABETH *and* BENNET *look at each other.* ELIZABETH *rises; crosses slowly to French windows; looks out. Pause.)*

MRS. BENNET. *(Sighs)* I'm sure I don't know why we should be having all this trouble.

BENNET. *(Dryly)* It seems to me that *Jane* has all the trouble, Mrs. Bennet. You have only the complaints. Have you heard how your daughter Lydia is going on at Brighton?

MRS. BENNET. Yes, that's another thing. Ever since she went there we've only had two letters. That's all your fault, Mr. Bennet.

BENNET. Your process of reasoning is too intricate for me, my dear. Evidently your daughter Lydia is enjoying herself— *(To* ELIZABETH*)* If I remember rightly, the last letter your mother received informed us that she and her friends had just returned from pacing the sea front, attended by a Mr. Wickham and other officers. *(At mention of* WICKHAM, ELIZABETH *gives a start; grasps back of chair* L.)

MRS. BENNET. *(Proudly. To* BENNET*)* Yes, the dear child is always surrounded. You have never done Lydia justice. You will see, she will make the best match of all my girls. *(As* ELIZABETH *sits* L.) That's sensible, my love. You've told me so little of your visit. How do the Collinses live? Very comfortably, I suppose. What sort of a table do they keep? I suppose Charlotte is an excellent manager? If she's as stingy as her mother, there won't be much wasted. Nothing extravagant in their housekeeping, I'll warrant.

ELIZABETH. I left before I had time to "investigate," Mama. You forget we only stayed at Rosings.

MRS. BENNET. *(Disappointedly)* Oh, yes, I forgot. Too bad! You can't tell me anything. I suppose when you were alone with them—in your rooms—they talked of how they should have Longbourn when your father is dead?

BENNET. I admire the composure with which you seem to face that inevitable prospect, Mrs. Bennet. Nevertheless, I wish you would not speak of me so constantly as a corpse. *(Rises; crosses to back of bench* R.) Let us hope for better things. Let us flatter ourselves that I may be the survivor.

MRS. BENNET. Well—if people can bring themselves to enjoy an estate that is not their own— (BENNET *crosses to door* R.C. MRS. BENNET *looks after him as he exits)* —so much the better— (BENNET *goes out of the door* R.C. *to* L.) Your father no doubt feels guilty whenever I refer to this matter.

ELIZABETH. *(Ironically)* Then would it not be kinder to spare his feelings, Mama?

MRS. BENNET. Yes, but men should be made to *feel* when they have done wrong. I don't hold with this trying to escape from responsibilities— (HILL *enters* R.C. *from* R.; *stands* R. *of door.)* —when one has daughters.

HILL. The Lady Catherine de Bourgh!

ELIZABETH. Lady Catherine? *(Rises.* MRS. BEN-NET *rises as* LADY CATHERINE *sweeps in, directly toward* ELIZABETH; *ignores* MRS. BENNET'S *greeting.* ELIZABETH, *curtseying)* Good afternoon, Your Ladyship. This is a pleasant surprise— *(Coldly polite.)*

MRS. BENNET. *(Fluttering toward her)* I am happy to receive Your Ladyship. *(Her tone syncophantic and affected. Curtseying.)*

LADY CATHERINE. *(Without turning to* MRS. BEN-NET, *simply looking at her over her shoulder)* This lady, I suppose, is your mother?

ELIZABETH. May I present my mother, Mrs. Bennet. Lady Catherine de Bourgh, Mama. (BOTH *ladies curtsey again*—MRS. BENNET *rather elaborately,* LADY CATHERINE *barely curtseys.)*

LADY CATHERINE. I noticed you have a very small park here. *(Crosses to French windows.)*

MRS. BENNET. *(Following her. Apologetically)* It's much larger than Sir William Lucas's. Has Your Ladyship lunched?

LADY CATHERINE. Certainly. At "The Jolly Millers" in Meryton. Do you suppose I should be uncertain about where I could procure my luncheon? I have more respect for my stomach, I hope, Mrs. Bennet. "The Jolly Millers" is as good an inn as any, and their cook is no doubt more efficient than the one you are likely to have in a place with such a very small park.

ELIZABETH. But of course, Lady Catherine—

LADY CATHERINE. I should like to converse with you alone, Miss Bennet.

MRS. BENNET. *(Fluttering. Backs away from* LADY CATHERINE *toward library door)* Certainly. I am most flattered at your kind interest in Lizzie—

If you need me, I shall be in the library—I'm reading a book. (ELIZABETH *crosses and opens library door.* MRS. BENNET *exits into library.* LADY CATHERINE *examines the room, pictures, etc.; crosses to table* L. *of small fireplace,* L., *tapping it with her lorgnette to see if it is genuine. Sits at fireplace* L.)

ELIZABETH. That piece is quite genuine—Lady Catherine. *(Crosses to* LADY CATHERINE*)* Is your chair comfortable?

LADY CATHERINE. Sit here— *(Indicates other chair in front of fireplace)* —Miss Bennet, where I can see you plainly. (ELIZABETH *does so.* LADY CATHERINE *eyes her an instant)* You know why I am here?

ELIZABETH. No, indeed, I don't know what I have done to deserve this honor.

LADY CATHERINE. Has not your conscience told you?

ELIZABETH. My *conscience?*

LADY CATHERINE. Miss Bennet, I am *not* to be trifled with. I am celebrated for my frankness. Don't assume those innocent airs—*I'm* not a man! They will have no affect whatever upon *me.* A report has reached me that you hope to be married to my nephew, Mr. Darcy. (ELIZABETH *shows complete surprise.)* I would not insult him by asking about the truth of this. I have come post haste from Rosings to let you know my exact sentiments.

ELIZABETH. What a long way to come for such a purpose, Lady Catherine. Especially as I know nothing of such a rumor.

LADY CATHERINE. Will you swear there is no foundation for it?

ELIZABETH. No, I do not pretend to be as celebrated for frankness as Your Ladyship. So there are certain questions I may not choose to answer—this is one of them.

LADY CATHERINE. How—how *dare* you? I insist on knowing! Has my nephew made you an offer of marriage?

ELIZABETH. But Your Ladyship has already declared that to be impossible.

LADY CATHERINE. It certainly *should be!* But your arts may have entangled him into forgetting what he owes to his family.

ELIZABETH. *(Rises, curtseys and steps away from her)* Then surely I should be the last to admit it.

LADY CATHERINE. *(Furiously, rising)* Miss Bennet, do you know *who* I am? I have not been accustomed— I am the nearest relative he has and entitled to know his dearest concerns.

ELIZABETH. *(Calmly)* Then question *him.* You certainly are not entitled to know *mine.*

LADY CATHERINE. This marriage to which you have the effrontery to aspire, will *never* take place. *Never!* Now what have you to say? *(Steps down to face* ELIZABETH.*)*

ELIZABETH. *(Placidly)* If there were no *other* objection to my marriage with Mr. Darcy—your commands would certainly carry little weight.

LADY CATHERINE. *(Crosses and sweeps by* ELIZABETH *to table* C.*)* Very well. If you persist—but don't expect to be received by his family—*or* his friends— *(Turns to* ELIZABETH*) Your name will never be mentioned by any of us!*

ELIZABETH. I must confess to Your Ladyship that this will not give me a moment's concern.

LADY CATHERINE. *(Amazed)* Miss Bennet, I am *ashamed* of you. *Is this* your gratitude for my hospitality?

ELIZABETH. *(Turns to her)* Gratitude! But, Lady Catherine, I regard hospitality as a mutual grace, and by no means consider myself an object for charity.

LADY CATHERINE. *(Coming down to* ELIZABETH ; *pacing about)* Understand, my girl, I came here determined— I am not used to submitting to any person's whims, nor brooking disappointments.

ELIZABETH. That is unfortunate. It is rather late in life for Your Ladyship to be receiving your first taste of it—

LADY CATHERINE. Be silent. The idea of you wanting to marry out of your own sphere!

ELIZABETH. *(Smiling)* Oh, I should not consider it so. Mr. Darcy is a gentleman—I am the daughter of one.

LADY CATHERINE. *(Coming to* ELIZABETH*)* And pray, what was your mother? A lady? *(Laughs scornfully)* The daughter of a shop-keeper, with a brother—an *attorney! !* (ELIZABETH *turns away from her)* You see, I am not deceived by your airs and graces.

ELIZABETH. *(Turns to her)* And you, Lady Catherine, the daughter of a peer! *(Stepping away from her)* It's strange how little birth seems to affect questions of taste—or— *(To* LADY CATHERINE*)* —gentleness of heart.

LADY CATHERINE. As if you could possibly know anything about such things. *(Crosses to* ELIZABETH*)* Answer me once and for all— *Are you engaged to my nephew?*

(MRS. LAKE *opens conservatory door; looks into living room in astonishment; makes a sign that there is too much noise.* ELIZABETH *nods.)*

ELIZABETH. I must ask you to speak in a lower key. My sister is asleep out there. *(Walks away from her; crosses* R. *to bench)* No, I am not engaged to him.

LADY CATHERINE. *(Crosses to sofa)* And will you promise me you never will be?

ELIZABETH. *(Turning to her; quietly)* I will not.

LADY CATHERINE. Miss Bennet, I am shocked!

(Pompously; sits on sofa) Then I refuse to leave until you have given me that promise.

ELIZABETH. *(Crosses to door R.C. and pulls bell cord)* I trust Your Ladyship will have a pleasant journey back to Rosings. (LADY CATHERINE *rises in amazement.* HILL *enters R.C. from L.)* Hill, Her Ladyship's coach, if you please.

HILL. It is waiting, Miss Lizzie.

LADY CATHERINE. *(Pauses in amazement as she crosses to door R.C.)* I take no leave of you. I send no farewell message to your mother! Miss Bennet, I am seriously displeased. (ELIZABETH *is making a curtsey as* LADY CATHERINE, *without returning it, stalks out R.C. to R., followed by* HILL, *who leaves the door open.* ELIZABETH, *shaking her head, comes down; crosses to fireplace R.; leans on mantel.* MRS. BENNET *comes in quickly from the library R. where she has probably tried to eavesdrop. Looking around room for* LADY CATHERINE.)

MRS. BENNET. *(Crosses to sofa)* Oh, why did Her Ladyship leave so soon? I had hoped to have a nice talk with her about the Collinses—

ELIZABETH. *(Crosses back of bench in front of fireplace R.)* She didn't wish to remain longer, Mama.

MRS. BENNET. *(On each question edges over closer to* ELIZABETH*)* She is a very fine-looking woman, my love—and her calling here was prodigiously civil— *(Hopefully)* She only came, I suppose, to tell us that the Collinses were well?—on her way somewhere, I daresay? *(Still hopeful of being told)* Passing through Meryton—thought she might as well call on you? *(A last attempt to find out)* I suppose she had nothing particular to say, Lizzie?

ELIZABETH. No, Mama—nothing at all. (MRS. BENNET *rises angrily at getting no information; crosses to chair R. of table C.* MR. BENNET'S *voice is heard off stage.)*

BENNET. *(As* MRS. BENNET *is at the chair C.)*

Lizzie! Lizzie! Where are you, Lizzie? Are you upstairs?

ELIZABETH. In here, Papa.

BENNET. *(Rushes in* R.C. *from* L. *to* ELIZABETH,
who meets him) Here, read this! *(Hands her letter.
Both* WOMEN *look up in alarm at his tone. He paces
up and down while* ELIZABETH *quickly reads.)*

MRS. BENNET. What is it, Mr. Bennet? You look
vexed about something?

ELIZABETH. Papa! This is frightful—

MRS. BENNET. I really think I am as deserving
of your confidence as my daughter Lizzie, Mr. Bennet. (ELIZABETH *is about to hand the letter to* MRS.
BENNET *when* BENNET *takes it from her.)*

BENNET. *(To* MRS. BENNET*)* Colonel Forster in-
forms me that your daughter Lydia has gone off with
Mr. Wickham.

MRS. BENNET. But where—?

BENNET. What does it matter where? The important thing is that she went anywhere with the
scoundrel! *(Down to her)* They have eloped—do
you understand? *(Paces up to door* R.C.; *stands
thinking.* MRS. BENNET *smiles at this, rather pleased.)*

ELIZABETH. *(Sits at* L. *end of sofa)* Wickham!
It seems incredible!

MRS. BENNET. *(Not grasping the true implica-
tion of the elopement)* Oh, the dear child—and without wedding clothes! Mr. Bennet, you must send
money at once—only how will she know what ware-
houses to choose? Lizzie, my love—I—

BENNET. *(Back to* MRS. BENNET, *interrupting
her)* They left Brighton at midnight on Saturday
and were not missed until eight o'clock yesterday
morning.

ELIZABETH. *(Anxiously)* But he will certainly
marry her, Papa?

MRS. BENNET. *(Rises.* ELIZABETH *also rises.)*

What? They are not married? Oh, that is impossible! My Lydia would not do such a thing!

BENNET. Kindly control yourself, Mrs. Bennet. This is no time for hysterics. Listen to this— *(Reads)* "Your daughter left a message for my wife stating that she and Mr. Wickham were gone to Gretna Green. I at once set off after them—and traced them as far as Clapham but there lost all clues; for on entering that place they removed into a hackney coach—"

MRS. BENNET. *(Begins to whimper)* Oh, my poor, innocent child!

ELIZABETH. *(Crosses to* MRS. BENNET*)* Mama! *(Embraces her.)*

BENNET. If you will restrain your outcries for just one moment until we ascertain the exact situation, then you may resume them again if you wish— *(Crosses to bench in front of* R. *fireplace.)*

MRS. BENNET. But how could she get married? She has no wedding clothes— *(This thought seems quite unendurable.)*

BENNET. *(Crosses back to* R.C., *quite exasperated)* Mrs. Bennet, for once in your life I entreat you to try not to be silly. (ELIZABETH *makes her a sign to be quiet.)* "All that is known after this is that they were seen to continue the London road. After making every possible inquiry on that side London, I am sincerely grieved to tell you— *(Slowly)* that I can find no further trace of them and no word—of any marriage ceremony—" (MRS. BENNET *emits a cry or wail.)*

ELIZABETH. Hush, Mama! *(Places her in the chair* C.*)* Colonel Forster's letter only says that he has found no trace of the ceremony yet— That doesn't mean—

BENNET. *(Pacing up and down* R.C. *Interrupting)* Whatever it means, you can rest assured that I will attend to that young man— *(Paces down to fireplace R. and back to R.C.)*

MRS. BENNET. *(Her hand to her heart)* Mr. Bennet, you frighten me out of my wits— *(Points to her heart.* ELIZABETH *soothes her.* MRS. BENNET *is now sobbing)* Oh, I know your father will fight Mr. Wickham and be killed— The Collinses will turn us out before he is cold in his grave.

ELIZABETH. Oh, do hush, Mama! (MRS. BENNET *is sobbing uncontrollably.)*

BENNET. *(Touched by her distress, goes to her)* There, there, my dear, don't be so upset. (ELIZABETH *crosses to bell pull; pulls it.)* We must all keep our heads. I'll help you upstairs, and Mrs. Lake will get you a sleeping potion.

ELIZABETH. Try to stand up, Mama. *(Comes back to* MRS. BENNET*)* I'll get Mrs. Lake— Papa and Hill will help you upstairs. (HILL *enters* R.C. *from* L. ELIZABETH *goes to door of conservatory, gently opens it, beckons to* MRS. LAKE, *who enters, closing it softly)* Mrs. Lake, will you prepare a potion for my mother? She is not well and needs some rest. (BENNET *helps his wife to her feet.* MRS. BENNET *leans against him whimperingly.* MRS. LAKE *takes her other arm and helps her off* R.C. *to* L.)

BENNET. *(To* HILL) Assist your mistress upstairs, then pack my bags quickly—

MRS. LAKE. I can manage alone, sir. *(To* MRS. BENNET*)* Lean on me, ma'am—that's the way— (MRS. BENNET *goes out, led by* MRS. LAKE, *whimpering like a child.* BENNET *crosses to fireplace* R., HILL *waiting respectfully for orders.)*

BENNET. Get the carriage ready. You'll drive me to the post house *(Looks at the watch; crosses to C.)* I'll catch the mail easily.

HILL. Yes, sir. *(Exits* R.C. *to* L.)

BENNET. *(Crosses to* ELIZABETH *by French win-*

dows. Looks at her anxiously) My child, I must
leave at once. Can you manage things here?

ELIZABETH. Of course, Papa.

BENNET. Don't you worry, I'll find them. I'll make
that scoundrel marry her—

ELIZABETH. Just get them married, Papa. Never
mind about punishing Wickham. But—how *could*
Lydia have done this?

BENNET. That shameless girl! She would have
eloped with anything in uniform.

ELIZABETH. It's our fault, mine especially. I had
been warned about Wickham. I could have saved
her. We never bothered about the poor child except
to criticize her.

BENNET. *(Takes her in his arms)* I too am to
blame—but my heart has it own bitternesss.

ELIZABETH. *(Low)* I know, Papa, dear, I know.

BENNET. *(Gently pats her head)* I'll say goodbye
to your mother and get my things.

MAID. *(Enters* R.C. *from* R.*)* Mr. Darcy, sir, and
Mr. Bingley. *(They enter* R.C. *from* R.*)*

DARCY. I hope we are not intruding, sir.

BENNET. Not at all, sir. You will excuse me, I am
posting up to London for a few days and must be
off. Goodbye, Lizzie. Take care of yourself.

ELIZABETH. Yes, Papa—I'll manage.

BENNET. *(Bowing)* Gentlemen!

DARCY *and* BINGLEY. Your servant, sir. (BENNET
goes out R.C. *to* L. BINGLEY *comes forward.)*

BINGLEY. Miss Elizabeth—may I be permitted to
see Miss Jane?

ELIZABETH. *(Resentful of* BINGLEY's *desertion)*
She is gravely ill, Mr. Bingley.

BINGLEY. I was shocked to hear it. I was told of
her illness only today. Mr. Darcy learned of it at
Rosings, and found me in London and brought me
here. I know that you and your family have every
reason to think ill of me, Miss Elizabeth, and I

shouldn't blame your sister if she refused ever to see me again. But there are some sentiments that are too strong to be denied or suppressed. Please do let me see her, Miss Elizabeth. I assure you I— *(Crosses to* Elizabeth. Elizabeth *looks at* Darcy. *A pause.)*

Elizabeth. I understand— She's out here. (Bingley *goes out through conservatory.* Elizabeth *shuts door after him and turns to face* Darcy. *Trying to speak in a cold tone)* Mr. Darcy—I find myself in the unexpected position of having to thank you—

Darcy. You need not embarrass yourself. I only beg that you will accept my word of honor that I had no idea that Miss Jane cared seriously for Charles. He knew no more of it than I. Miss Bingley assured us both that your sister had only a passing interest in him.

Elizabeth. Miss Bingley formed her own opinion too readily—as I did in my judgment of Mr. Wickham. *(She comes down to* Darcy, r. *of chair* c.) Mr. Darcy—you must tell me what you know of him! *(She is so urgent in this request that* Darcy *looks at her curiously.)*

Darcy. *(Takes step to* Elizabeth*)* You care for him!

Elizabeth. No! But it's very important that I know the real truth about him.

Darcy. Part of the story he tells is true. He was granted a small legacy in my father's will. I saw that this was more than fulfilled. I gave him three thousand pounds and the offer of the clerical living at Pemberly. He haughtily refused the living but graciously accepted the money. It was squandered within a year, thanks to Mr. Wickham's ill luck in gambling and his fascination for women. He was driven to more desperate measures—he learned that my sister was at Ramsgate—

Elizabeth. Mr. Wickham—and *your* sister?

DARCY. He persuaded that child of fifteen that she was in love with him and made her promise to elope. Thank God I arrived in time to spoil the plan.

ELIZABETH. *(Comes to front of chair c.)* Oh—if I had only listened to you. I might have saved Lydia.

DARCY. Lydia?

ELIZABETH. She was staying at Brighton with the Forsters. She eloped from there. That's why my father has just gone up to London. He will never marry her! She has no money, no connections, nothing to tempt him! Lydia is done for.

DARCY. Please, you must not despair!

ELIZABETH. You see, my family is not only inferior—but disgraced now. You should be grateful to me. *(BINGLEY and MRS. LAKE appear at French windows.)*   *(WARN Curtain.)*

BINGLEY. *(Enters)* And may I come again tomorrow to see her? *(ELIZABETH crosses down to him.)*

MRS. LAKE. *(Smiling)* Indeed you may, sir. *(She shuts the door after him and goes off L.)*

BINGLEY. *(Comes down)* Thank you, thank you, Miss Elizabeth.

ELIZABETH. And you *will* see her again tomorrow?

BINGLEY. I hope I shall see her on every tomorrow that may ever be. *(He kisses ELIZABETH's hand.)*

DARCY. *(Somewhat stiffly)* I must bid you good-bye, Miss Elizabeth. I am leaving Netherfield at once—

BINGLEY. *(Crosses to DARCY)* But I thought you were to stay on with us for—

DARCY. I find it impossible to stay on.

BINGLEY. But what has caused this sudden change? Has anything gone wrong?

DARCY. You know I have no taste for life in the country.

BINGLEY. *(Looks from DARCY to ELIZABETH, wondering what has happened)* I'm sorry— Good-bye, Miss Elizabeth.

ELIZABETH. *(Takes step to* BINGLEY. *He kisses her hand.)* Goodbye, Mr. Bingley. (BINGLEY *goes out* R.C. *to* R.) Goodbye, Mr. Darcy.

DARCY. Your servant, ma'am. *(He bows and goes* R.C. *to* R.)

ELIZABETH. *(Looks after him for a moment, then turns to the conservatory. She runs to the door and opens it)* Jane! Jane! My darling—

CURTAIN

SCENE II

SCENE: *The same. Two weeks later. Morning.*
A beautiful morning in May. Mullioned windows open, curtains fluttering, sunshine pouring in, flowers everywhere, especially big sprays of hawthorn, masses of spirea and honeysuckle in bowls.

AT RISE: JANE *is propped up on sofa, radiant with happiness and returning health.*
MRS. BENNET *is C., sewing on a trousseau for* JANE'S *forthcoming wedding, with a happy smile on her lips. No one speaks for a while, each occupied with their thoughts.*

JANE. *(After watching her mother)* Isn't it wonderful to be alive on such a morning, Mama?

MRS. BENNET. *(With a birdlike glance at* JANE*)* Yes, indeed! Even the weather seems to be celebrating your engagement with that dear Bingley, my love. *(Giggles girlishly)* Dear me, I must learn to call him Charles now that he is to be my son. You know, Jane, I can scarce sleep o' nights for happiness.

JANE. *(Tenderly)* Dear Mama!

MRS. BENNET. Two sons-in-law! Both my daughters to be married women! How proud I feel, to be sure! Lydia already married to that naughty Mr. Wickham! Your father certainly managed all that business very well. If it were not for Lizzie! I cannot bear her to turn out to be an old maid. If only she had not been so uppish with that young Collins! *(Sighs.)*

BENNET. *(Entering* R.C. *from* L. *Stands in doorway listening to* MRS. BENNET*)* Well, let's hope it will be a lesson to her! *(Chuckles. Surveying the furbelows* MRS. BENNET *is sewing)* Marriages in the air, I see! *(Glances at flowers everywhere)* Two in the family! Completely restored you to health, eh, Mrs. Bennet? *(Crosses to* JANE; *bends down to her)* You too, Jane, your old self again. When does Mr. Bingley arrive?

JANE. He'll be here any moment now, Papa.

BENNET. That friend of his, Mr. Darcy, is a very extraordinary young man! *(Sees* ELIZABETH *come to the door through conservatory, carrying flowers, and continues for her benefit)* We've seen quite a lot of him at the Gardiner's while I was in London.

ELIZABETH. *(Places some flowers on table* C.*)* Darcy? Darcy at the Gardiners?

JANE. *(Triumphantly)* You see, Lizzie, you thought him so proud! I told you you misjudged him.

MRS. BENNET. Oh, Lizzie thinks she knows more than everybody else—

ELIZABETH. Oh, no—Mama! Not everybody— *(Mischievously looking at mother.)*

MRS. BENNET. *(Sighs. Regarding her thoughtfully)* Of course you're only twenty—though to be sure I was married to Mr. Bennet when I was seventeen.

BENNET. But remember how irresistible you were, my dear? (MRS. BENNET *giggles happily.)*

ELIZABETH. *(Crosses to table* L., *below fireplace)* Don't despair, Mama. While there's life there's hope. And after all, I've still some of my teeth. (JANE *laughs.)*

MRS. BENNET. You shouldn't joke about such things, my dear! You know, Lizzie, you can't expect your papa to find another ten thousand to give to you—or your Uncle Gardiner— He, I understand, found the sum for us— *(As an afterthought)* though I earnestly hope he doesn't expect us to pay it back.

ELIZABETH. *(Crosses to table* C.*)* I didn't know my uncle could spare so much money— *(Puzzled.)*

MRS. BENNET. Anyway, I'm glad *someone* in the family was able to find the money for darling Lydia's dowry.

ELIZABETH. *(Dryly)* Otherwise, no doubt, "the naughty Mr. Wickham" would have continued to live in sin with her. *(Takes rest of flowers to table.)*

MRS. BENNET. *Lizzie!* Your *own* sister! If the servants were to hear you!

BENNET. But isn't that the accepted way of mentioning a young lady and gentleman who are travelling about in post-chaises together without benefit of clergy?

MRS. BENNET. There is *no* way of mentioning it—not for respectable people.

ELIZABETH. My poor Uncle Gardiner had to spend ten thousand pounds so that respectable people *could mention* it. I only hope he has not sacrificed the principal of his fortune for this worthless pair.

BENNET. You can dismiss that worry from your mind, Lizzie.

ELIZABETH. *(Looks at him, puzzled)* What do you mean, Papa?

MRS. BENNET. Oh, my good kind brother! I knew he would manage everything.

ELIZABETH. *(Crosses to* R. *of* MRS. BENNET. *Reflectively. Slowly)* But—ten—thousand—pounds!

MRS. BENNET. Well, it's none of your business, Lizzie. Lydia is married and secured. That's all that matters—

ELIZABETH. *(Contemplating her mother)* Cannibals and brigands are *gentle*—in comparison—

MRS. BENNET. *(Wonderingly)* In comparison? With what!

ELIZABETH. *(Crosses to back of sofa)* Mothers. (MRS. BENNET *looks at* ELIZABETH, *puzzled.*)

BENNET. *(Pauses. Slowly crosses to front of bench* R.; *sits on it)* Ah! Did I mention that it was through Mr. Darcy's efforts we found the pair—

ELIZABETH. What?　　　　⎫
JANE. Mr. Darcy!　　　　⎬ *(Simultaneously.)*
MRS. BENNET. That man!　⎭

BENNET. And— *(Pretends·not to observe* ELIZABETH'S *start)* —that he obtained the money for us— to buy back Lydia's—respectability?

ELIZABETH. It's not true.　　　　⎫
JANE. Papa.　　　　　　　　　　⎬ *(Simultaneously.)*
MRS. BENNET. You're joking,　　⎭
Mr. Bennet.

JANE. He must be a noble character.

ELIZABETH. But *why* should Mr. Darcy do all this?

MRS. BENNET. I understand that he detests Mr. Wickham. And he has never been at all nice to my daughter Lydia. *(Frowns)* I should have preferred my brother Gardiner to have paid the money. Why didn't he, Mr. Bennet?

BENNET. For the very simple reason, Mrs. Bennet, that he hasn't got it. (ELIZABETH *crosses to chair down* R.) As to why Mr. Darcy played the philanthropist, that will probably be revealed in its own good time. *(Sternly)* But remember, Lydia and Wickham are *never* to know!

MRS. BENNET. You needn't worry about *me* ever telling— I prefer Mr. Wickham to believe that members of our family provided his wife's dowry. Then when I wish to visit my girl, he can never object.

BENNET. *(Gazes at her in wonder at such cunning combined with simplicity.* ELIZABETH *smiles.)* Did

I mention that your daughter and her new husband are being sent to join his regiment up North? They will arrive here today on their way there.

MRS. BENNET. Oh! Mr. Bennet!

BENNET. *(Rises)* I am not at all decided to receive the Wickhams here, Mrs. Bennet.

MRS. BENNET. What!

JANE. Oh, we must receive them, Papa!

MRS. BENNET. Yes.

JANE. Lydia has injured herself enough without being cast off by us.

BENNET. Well, perhaps you are right.

MRS. BENNET. Oh, how wonderful it will be to see my Lydia again.

HILL. *(Enters* R.C. *from* R.*)* Mr. Charles Bingley!

MRS. BENNET. *(Rises to greet him as soon as* HILL *announces* BINGLEY*)* Oh, do come in, my dear Mr. Bingley!

BINGLEY. *(Entering; kissing her hand; his eye roving at once for* JANE*)* Your servant, ma'am. *(Crosses to* BENNET*)* And yours, sir. *(Crosses to front of sofa and* BENNET *bows to him)* My sister sends greetings to you all from Netherfield and to you especially. *(Sits on sofa; bends down tenderly; kisses* JANE'S *hand.)*

JANE. Please convey mine to her.

MRS. BENNET. How charming! Everything just as it used to be.

BINGLEY. Not quite, ma'am. I'm hoping, you know, to have a new mistress there very soon. *(Rises; to* BENNET*)* I came over today, sir, for your consent— You received my letter in London?

BENNET. My boy, you are the first suitor for any of my daughters who has met with my approval— With all my heart, sir! *(Shakes hands.* ELIZABETH *crosses to* BINGLEY*; clasps his hands. He kisses her hand.* MRS. BENNET *crosses to* BINGLEY, *arms outstretched; tears him away from* ELIZABETH*; kisses* *him; turns to* JANE; *kisses her. Sits on sofa and pulls* BINGLEY *down to her. She holds both their hands.* BENNET *crosses to* JANE, *back of sofa)* You are a good girl, Jane. I am happy to see you will have a husband worthy of you. I have not a single doubt about the success of this marriage. *(Eyes the pair with smiling irony)* You are too much alike not to agree. You are both so sweet-tempered that your servants will always impose on you. *(Laughs as they do also.* ELIZABETH *sits on bench.)* And so generous that you will always exceed your income. *(Kisses* JANE *on forehead)* Bless you, my children!

MRS. BENNET. *(Literally)* Mr. B., you *do* say the queerest things. My daughter Jane has never been extravagant, and as for exceeding their income—dear Charles has five thousand a year. That ought to be enough to keep them from the almshouse. *(Giggles and clasps their hands to her bosom.)*

JANE. *(Quickly)* Mama, don't you think I could go for a walk with Charles in the garden? (MRS. BENNET *exits* R.C. *to* R.)

HILL. *(Off stage)* Oh, Miss Lydia—I mean Mrs. Wickham.

ELIZABETH. It's Lydia! *(Crosses to* L.C.)

MRS. BENNET. *(Off)* Lydia! Lydia! My darling child! And Mr. Wickham! Allow me to greet my first son-in-law!

LYDIA. *(Off)* Oh, Mama—such a journey as we have had—

WICKHAM. *(Off. Airily)* Terribly tedious, indeed! How is my new family? *(Those inside the room stare at each other.)*

LYDIA. *(They enter* R.C. *from* R.) Well, congratulate me. I'm a married woman now. *(Crosses to* JANE. WICKHAM *gives a general bow to* JANE *and* BINGLEY, *then crosses to* ELIZABETH.)

JANE. Welcome, Lydia dear.

LYDIA. Ah, Jane, dear, and Charles.

WICKHAM. Have you seen any of our friends in Meryton, Miss Elizabeth?

ELIZABETH. I have not, Mr. Wickham.

WICKHAM. Now—I—may be less formal—Lizzie.

ELIZABETH. That is hardly necessary.

LYDIA. *(Crosses to* ELIZABETH*)* Lizzie, my child! *(Kisses her.)*

ELIZABETH. Lydia!

LYDIA. *(To* BENNET, *who has ignored her)* Did you have a nice journey back from London, Papa? We left quite soon after you—there was plenty of room in our chaise for you, wasn't there, Mr. Wickham?

WICKHAM. We should have been honored— (BENNET *merely regards her gravely. Crosses up* C.)

LYDIA. Only think—it's three whole months since I went away— *(Looks around)* Just the same old place— Good gracious, I certainly had no idea of being married when I left. *(Crosses to* L. *of table* C. ; *leans over the table* C. ; *to* MRS. BENNET*)* Oh, Mama, do the people hereabouts know I'm married? *(Giggles.)*

WICKHAM. *(Smugly)* Of course, my dear, everyone knows it.

LYDIA. Do you know what happened on our way down? Our chaise overtook William Goulding in his curricle. I was determined he should know—I mean about my being married. So what do you think I did? *(Chuckles)* As *our* coach passed his, I let down the window—the one next to him—and rested my hand on the window frame—like this— *(Holds ring hand out affectedly)* —so that he'd see my wedding ring! The whole of Meryton will know it by now. Then I bowed and smiled—like this— *(Does it to show them. Crosses to* JANE*)* Ah, my lady, you can still be the prettiest if you like, but I'm the one who got married first. (BENNET *stares at* LYDIA; *stalks out of the room* R.C. *to* R. *in disgust.* LYDIA, *giving a gamin grin at her father's disappearing back, walks over to* WICKHAM; *takes his arm. They* BOTH *take a step* C.) And what do you all think of my new husband? I'm sure you two girls must envy me. Isn't he charming?

WICKHAM. You embarrass me, Mrs. Wickham!

LYDIA. I only hope they have half my good luck! They must both go to Brighton, That's the place to find husbands. (ELIZABETH *crosses to* L.C.)

MRS. BENNET. *(Also oblivious of the atmosphere. Plaintively)* But, Lydia, darling, must you and Mr. Wickham live so far away?

LYDIA. *(Airily)* Why not? I'm going to love it. *(And patronizingly.* ELIZABETH *crosses back of* LYDIA *and* WICKHAM *and toward library.)* You and Papa and Sisters must come visit me. We shall be at New Castle all next winter, and I daresay there will be some balls. I'll see that the girls get some good partners, you leave it to me. I'll find husbands for them before the winter's over.

ELIZABETH. Thank you for your kind intentions. But I don't particularly care for your way of getting husbands. *(Exits into library* R.)

LYDIA. *(With a scornful laugh)* La! Jealousy is a dreadful feeling. Poor Lizzie! *(Crosses to* JANE) I'm glad, Jane, that *you* at any rate are not cross at me at my getting a husband before you. (JANE *is silent. There is another uncomfortable silence which even* MRS. BENNET *notices.)*

WICKHAM. Ah, but perhaps your sister Jane will be able to follow your example very soon. (BINGLEY *rises; crosses to fireplace.)*

LYDIA. I was the first, at any rate.

MRS. BENNET. *(Crosses to* WICKHAM) Lydia, my love, take Mr. Wickham upstairs. You'll both need to prepare for luncheon—you can't leave before that— *(Crosses with them to door* R.C.)

LYDIA. *(Turns to* JANE*)* Don't we make a nice couple, Jane? *(As she and* WICKHAM *exit* R.C. *to* L.*)*

MRS. BENNET. Take Jane for a little sunshine in the garden, Charles. You must excuse my Lydia— she's so young. *(In the* R.C. *doorway.)*

BINGLEY. *(Crosses front of sofa)* I am delighted to see her so happy, ma'am. (MRS. BENNET *exits* R.C. *to* L. *To* JANE) My darling— *(She rises. They embrace. Kisses her. They start toward conservatory)* I can't believe this—

JANE. Is it more difficult to believe this than what you believed in London?

BINGLEY. Jane, you knew I loved you when I left Netherfield.

JANE. Ah, yes, but I had that knowledge all entirely to myself— *(Smiling)* It's only value is when it is mutual—

BINGLEY. But I was assured of your indifference, my darling.

JANE. *(Demurely)* That, sir, is a credit to your modesty rather than to your judgment.

BINGLEY. If I had only known— *(Takes her in his arms.)*

JANE. *(Softly)* If you had only asked— (DARCY *enters* R.C. *from* R., *followed by* BENNET. JANE *rises.)*

BINGLEY. My dear fellow— I didn't know—

JANE. Mr. Darcy— *(Curtseying)* —please wish me joy— It's your doing, you know. *(Comes down toward him, holding out both her hands with a charming gesture.)*

DARCY. *(Taking both her hands)* Words wouldn't do it for me, my dear Miss Jane. I wish you both— every happiness. *(Releases her hand; shakes hands with* BINGLEY. JANE *and* BINGLEY *go out hand in hand through conservatory.* DARCY *quickly crosses to library door as* MRS. BENNET *appears in door* R.C. *Seeing* DARCY *she gives an annoyed exclamation. His back is toward her.* BENNET *takes her by the shoul-*

ders, whispers something, gently propels her out R.C.
to L. *as she gives a gurgle of delight and a backward
look of amazement at* DARCY, *who is now knocking on
library door.* BENNET *gets her out, closes door
gently on himself and her.* DARCY *crosses, surpised
to see* C. *doors closed)* Now don't let us keep you
from your walk.

ELIZABETH. *(In response to* DARCY'S *knock, appears; stands in the doorway.* DARCY *hears her come
in; turns to her.)* You? I did not expect— *(Her
voice trembles in spite of her desire to appear cold.)*

DARCY. *(Humbly)* I hope I am not altogether un-
welcome?

ELIZABETH. *(Crosses to* R. *of sofa, trying to sound
cold and reserved)* I am glad of the opportunity—
of expressing my gratitude for all you have done—
for all of us.   *(WARN Curtain.)*

DARCY. Let it be for yourself alone—for whatever I did—I thought only of you.

ELIZABETH. Of *me?*

DARCY. *(Crosses to* L. *end of sofa; humbly)* Miss
Elizabeth, you are too generous to trifle with me—
(She looks surprised.) I came to ask you if you con-
tinue to feel towards me as you did at Rosings?

ELIZABETH. I could not imagine that such matters
still concerned you, sir.

DARCY. *(With grave simplicity) That* matter—
will always concern me, Miss Elizabeth. *(She shakes
her head. He comes closer)* Can you ever forget
my past arrogance?

ELIZABETH. *(Smiling a little tearfully)* Surely in
such a case a good memory would be unpardonable?

DARCY. *(Smiles at this flash of the old* ELIZABETH.
They suddenly look a little tremulously at each other)
Elizabeth!

ELIZABETH. I am so ashamed! *(Her head down.
A tear glistens on her cheek. The sight fills him with
tenderness.)* If you had not been noble and just, you

would have hated me. (ELIZABETH *shakes her head)* I was the stupid one—the foolishly proud one.

DARCY. *(Tenderly)* No, my dearest—only the prejudiced one—

ELIZABETH. *(Turns away from him)* When I think of the way you requited my incivility—my cruelty— *(Brokenly)* Oh—I cannot bear your kindness—-

DARCY. *(Steps closer to her)* But if all these things you so exaggerate had been done by your husband? *(Softly.)*

ELIZABETH. *(Turns to him)* Enjoy your triumph! *(With bowed head)* I am abased! I never wanted to see you again!

DARCY. *(Pause)* Do you still mean that?

ELIZABETH. *(A pause. Begins to say "yes" but bows her head; shakes it)* No!

DARCY. Dare I ask you again?—Again?

ELIZABETH. *(Smiles up at him through her tears)* My father says you are the sort of gentleman one would not dare refuse anything he condescended to ask— *(Puts her head on his shoulder.)*

DARCY. My cruel—my kind—oh, my lovely Elizabeth!

CURTAIN

PRIDE AND PREJUDICE

INCIDENTAL MUSIC

Overture:
- (1) English Harvesters' Dance (Old English Folk Song).
- (2) English Country Dance (Sir Roger de Coverly).
- (3) The Fair-Haired Maiden, by Thomas Moore (1779-1852).
- (4) The Dashing White Sergeant, by H. R. Bishop (1786-1855).
- (5) The Plough Boy (Old English Folk Song).

Stage:

Quadrille:
- (1) Rondo, by W. A. Mozart (20" first part; 15" second part).
  Oberon, by C. M. v. Weber (15").
  Rondo, by Joseph Haydn (40").
  Freischutz (Jagerchor) by C. M. v. Weber (40").
- (2) Walzer, by John Field (1782-1837) (1', 50").
- (3) Menuet (Don Juan), by W. A Mozart (1').
- (4) Walzer (Freischutz) by C. M. v. Weber (1', 05").
- (5) Walzer, by J. B. Cramer (1771-1858) (2' 10").
- (6) Gavotte, by F. J. Gosse (1734-1829) (1', 55").

(7) Gavotte, by J. B. Lully (1633-1687) (1′, 30″).

(8) Waltz (no. 1) by C. M. v. Weber (1786-1826) (1′, 55″).

(9) Gavotte, by Mehul (1763-1817) (0′, 55″).

Entra' Act I.

(1) Cut.

(2) Menuett, by Chr. W. v. Gluck (1711-1787).

(3) Bourres, by J. L. Krebs (1713-1780).

(4) Menuett, by Milandre (1770).

(5) Waltz (No. 2) C. M. v. Weber.

(6) Menuetto, by W. A. Mozart.

(7) Gigue, by Greery.

Entra' Act II.

(1) Waltzer, by J. M. Hummel (1778-1837).

(2) Drink to me only with thine eyes (Old English Air) by Ben Johnson (1573-1637).

(3) Menuetto (Aus dem D-dur Divertomento) W. A. Mozart.

(4) Plaisir d'Amour (Romance) G. B. Martini

(5) Rondino (On a Theme by Bethoven), Fritz Kreisler.

(6) Londonerry Air (Old Irish Melody).

Finale:

The Dashing White Sergeant, by H. R. Bishop (1786-1855).

PRIDE AND PREJUDICE

PROPERTY PLOT

Furniture:
  1 green upholstered sofa.
  1 gray upholstered sofa.
  1 gold empire couch.
  2 cane seated armchairs with red cushions.
  1 small bench with red cushion.
  1 green damask-upholstered wing chair.
  2 armchairs upholstered in green plush.
  2 armchairs upholstered in gray moire.
  1 empire drop front desk.
  1 wire front commode.
  1 spinet.
  1 stool with yellow leather top.
  4 armchairs in yellow damask.
  2 large armchairs in yellow damask.
  1 column commode.
  1 check top table.
  1 table with green and white top.
  1 drum table with leather top.
  1 painted green open front console table.
  1 small sewing stand.
  1 drop leaf table.
  2 green marbleized top console tables.
  2 green marbleized top round tables.
  1 white fern stand.
  4 yellow fern stands.
  2 black, white and gold empire stands.

1 all over gray carpet.

Curtains:

    3 celanese glass curtains.

    1 pair celanese draw curtains.

    1 pair gray satin drapes with valance and tie backs.

    5 gilt and glass curtain holders.

    6 small rods.

    5 painted blinds.

    Yellow net curtain drapery with valance and glass beads.

Silver plate, etc.

    2 sheffield candlesticks.

    1 short sheffield candlestick and snuffer.

    1 silver and crystal ink well.

    1 sheffield card salver.

    2 large sheffield tea trays.

    2 sheffield trays.

    1 small, oblong silver plated tray.

    3 sheffield teapots.

    2 sheffield cream jugs.

    2 sheffield sugar bowls.

    2 sheffield sugar tongs.

    1 sheffield punch bowl.

    18 sterling silver goblets.

Lighting Fixtures:

    2 tall gilt oil lamps and glass shades.

    1 double oil lamp (brass and crystal).

    1 double light candlestand with two glass shades.

    2 fire grates with coals.

Bric a brac, etc.:

    2 pewter measures.

    1 covered pewter jar.

    1 hanging shelf (in two sections).

    2 small silver urns.

    1 shell ink well.

    2 gilt figurines.

    1 blue glass box.

1 petit point tray.
2 crystal candelabra (3 light).
2 green pottery urns.
2 painted tine vases.
1 small clock with gilt figurine.
1 large gilt clock with bronge figure.
2 large gilt barometers.
2 large gilt candelabra on marble bases (6 lights each).
2 gilt wall sconces (3 lights each).
2 large porcelain urns.
1 blue pottery vase.
Small Properties:
4 yellow teacups and saucers.
8 blue teacups and saucers.
1 double tiered cake plate.
1 single tiered cake plate.
2 embroidery frames and embroidery.
12 teaspoons.
70 leather bound books.
1 sewing basket and spools, needles, etc.
1 prop hat (sewing).
2 candle snuffers.
1 dresden china candelabra.
2 sets fire irons (6 pieces each).
1 wooden coal bucket.
1 chintz coverd writing case.
1 hand bell.
1 chime.
1 white veil (prop sewing).
Copies of the *London Times* (1805).
5 rubber stamps (post mark cancellations).
Pictures:
1 large painting—man in yellow wig.
1 large painting of a woman.
1 portrait of a man in red coat.
1 large painting of man (full length).
4 gray tempera paintings.

1 silhouette in walnut frame.
1 green lustre and marble placque.
2 small oil paintings of Grecian figures.
Flowers.
4 boxes filled with fern.
4 boxes filled with tulips and marigolds.
2 bunches hawthorn.
2 white vases filled with forsythia and yellow
larkspur.
Ivy on conservatory backing (Act I).
Grape vine on arbor backing (Act II).
1 bunch yellow flowers.
1 bunch blue flowers.
1 bunch white flowers.

PRIDE AND PREJUDICE

COSTUME PLOT

MRS. BENNET:
> 1 blue and white and yellow costume.
> 1 white satin evening gown.
> 1 black and white challie.
> 1 golden brown dress.
> 1 gold dress, black lace apron.
> Caps, bags, fan, shoes.
> 1 wig.

ELIZABETH:
> 1 green and white dress—green velvet jacket.
> 1 red evening gown with scarf.
> 1 grey and red dress with scarf.
> 1 figured challie with scarf.
> 1 white dress—green dots with a scarf.
> 1 white and brick color dress.
> Ribbons for hair, bags, fan, shoes.
> Lots of hair.

LADY DE BOURGH:
> 1 brown and gold dress, hat, parasol, yellow
> gloves.
> 1 green moire, blue lace scarf.
> Large hat with blue lace bag.
> Parasol, gloves, green shoes.
> 2 red wigs.

MRS. GARDINER:
> 1 grey embroidered satin gown.
> Long black silk coat.
> Bonnet.

LADY LUCAS:
>   1 green striped dress, bonnet, cape, gloves.
>   1 garnet dress, hat, gloves.
>   Grey and black large scarf.
>   Grey curls.

JANE:
>   1 yellow dress.
>   1 white and silver dress.
>   1 blue flannel dress with scarf.
>   1 yellow and white silk dress.
>   1 brown velvet jacket and hat.
>   1 peach and black dress and scarf.
>   Curls.

LYDIA:
>   1 tan dress.
>   1 blue and grey dress, blue plaid shoes.
>   1 tan silk dress with embroidery.
>   1 grey dress with blue jacket and bonnet.
>   Parasol, black lace gloves.
>   Curls.

CHARLOTTE:
>   1 figured dress hat, muff red and white shoes.
>   1 green satin evening gown, silver scarf.
>   1 peach dress with black and white jacket.
>   Bonnet, parasol—black and white.
>   Curls.

AGATHA:
>   1 green and white silk dress and headdress.
>   Black moire cape, mitts.
>   1 blue Maid dress for MAGGIE, mitts.
>   Bangs.

AMANDA:
>   1 yellow crepe dress with headdress.
>   White mitts, green scarf.

BELINDA:
>   1 blue satin train dress.
>   1 grey scarf, white mitts, headdress.
>   Curls.

AMELIA.
> 1 green moire dress, yellow scarf, white mitts.
> Curls.

BENNET MAID:
> 1 black Maid dress, gingham apron, cap and
> pleated collar.
> Curls.

MISS BINGLEY:
> 1 grey evening gown and cloak, black gloves.
> 1 tan dress, green velvet jacket.
> Bonnet, tan gloves.
> Hair back.

MRS. LAKE:
> 1 blue flannel dress and apron.
> 2 hats, 2 pleated collars.

MR. DARCY:
> 3 pair pants.
> 4 coats.
> 5 vests.
> 1 long black cloak.
> 1 extra pair yellow pants.
> 1 black hat.
> 1 pair brown gloves.
> 1 pair patton pumps.
> 1 pair monocles.
> 2 pair drawers.
> 2 pair silk socks.
> 1 pair white gloves.
> 3 white stocks.
> 1 riding whip.
> 1 pair boots.

MR. BENNET:
> 3 pair pants.
> 3 coats.
> 3 vests.
> 1 long green coat (1st Act).
> 1 high hat.
> 1 wig.

1 stock.
1 riding whip.
1 pair boots.
2 pair shots, elastic sides, 1 old pair.
1 pair red slippers.
2 silk handkerchiefs.
2 pair socks.
1 pair wool gloves.
1 watch.

Mr. Collins:
2 black coats.
1 gray coat.
1 pair gray pants.
1 pair gray pants (extra).
1 pair white gloves.
1 silk handkerchief.
1 pair white socks.
1 high hat.
2 pair shoes.
1 white stock.
2 pair socks.

Mr. Bingley:
3 coats.
4 vests.
2 pair pants.
1 riding whip.
1 black long cloak.
1 black hat.
1 pair boots.
1 pair patton pumps.
1 pair white gloves.
1 pair brown gloves.
1 scarf.
1 pair stockings.
2 stocks.

Fitzwilliam:
1 military red coat.
1 pair plaid pants.

1 pair plaid pants (extra).
1 plaid sash.
1 white leather belt.
1 gold sash.
1 monocle.
1 pair elastic boots.
1 pair wool socks.
1 jock strap.
1 white stock.

MR. WICKHAM:

1 military red coat.
2 pair pants.
2 white stocks.
1 pair high boots.
1 pair elastic boots.
1 white belt.
1 sword.

HILL:

1 black coat.
2 pair pants.
1 pair shoes.
1 stock.
2 vests.
2 pair stockings.

CAPTAIN DENNY:

1 red coat, military.
1 pair pants.
1 white stock.
1 white belt.
1 sword.
1 pair elastic boots.
1 pair white gloves.
1 hat, not in use.

2ND YOUNG MAN:

1 black coat.
1 white pants.
1 long black cloak.

    1 black hat.
    1 white vest.
1ST YOUNG MAN:
    1 black coat.
    1 pair white pants.
    1 long black coat.
    1 black hat.
    1 white vest.

122

CYCLORAMA

GARDEN

PLATFORM

FRENCH

WINDOWS

FIREPLACE

STAND

ARM CHAIR

CHAIR

TABLE

CHAIR

SPINET

STOOL

CABINET

HALLWAY

DOOR RC

TABLE

DOOR R

DESK

LAMP

BENCH

SOFA

FIRE PLACE

INTERIOR

SCENE DESIGN
ACT I
ACT 2-SCENE I
ACT 3
PRIDE AND PREJUDICE

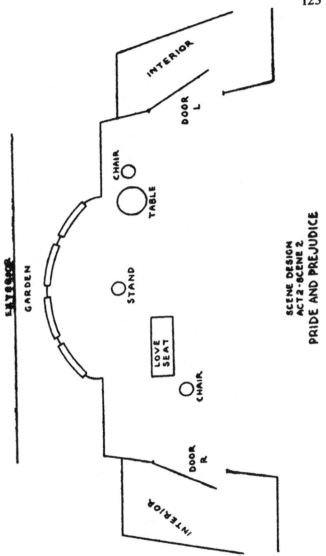

EXTERIOR

GARDEN

INTERIOR

DOOR L

CHAIR

TABLE

STAND

LOVE SEAT

CHAIR

DOOR R

INTERIOR

SCENE DESIGN
ACT 2-SCENE 2
PRIDE AND PREJUDICE

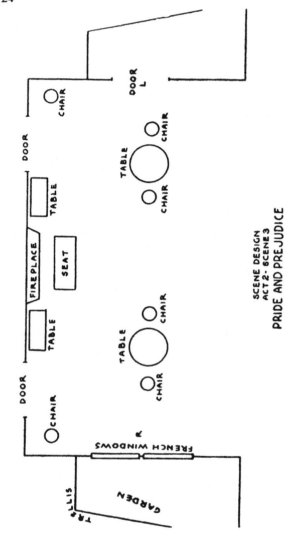

SCENE DESIGN
ACT 2 - SCENE 3
PRIDE AND PREJUDICE

TREASURE ISLAND
Ken Ludwig

All Groups / Adventure / 10m, 1f (doubling) / Areas
Based on the masterful adventure novel by Robert Louis Steven-
son, *Treasure Island* is a stunning yarn of piracy on the tropical
seas. It begins at an inn on the Devon coast of England in 1775
and quickly becomes an unforgettable tale of treachery and
mayhem featuring a host of legendary swashbucklers including
the dangerous Billy Bones (played unforgettably in the movies
by Lionel Barrymore), the sinister two-timing Israel Hands, the
brassy woman pirate Anne Bonney, and the hideous form of evil
incarnate, Blind Pew. At the center of it all are Jim Hawkins, a
14-year-old boy who longs for adventure, and the infamous Long
John Silver, who is a complex study of good and evil, perhaps the
most famous hero-villain of all time. Silver is an unscrupulous
buccaneer-rogue whose greedy quest for gold, coupled with his
affection for Jim, cannot help but win the heart of every soul
who has ever longed for romance, treasure and adventure.

9 780573 614262